Evil's Echo

Also by Jane Alden

The Payback Murders

The Crystal's Curse

Jobyna's Blues

Across A Crowded Room

Evil's Echo

Jane Alden

Desert Palm Press

Evil's Echo

By Jane Alden

©2022 Jane Alden

ISBN (book): 9781954213555
ISBN (epub): 9781954213562

Desert Palm Press
1961 Main Street, Suite 220
Watsonville, California 95076
www.desertpalmpress.com

Editor: Heather Flournoy
Cover Design: TreeHouse Studio

Printed in the United States of America
First Edition December 2022

Acknowledgements

Many thanks to beta readers Jazzy Mitchell, Molly Lovelock, Patricia Clark, and Jennifer Dawson, and a special thank you to publisher Lee Fitzsimmons of Desert Palm Press, editor Heather Flournoy, and cover artist Ann McMan. I hope readers enjoy meeting Butch Tracy, crime reporter.

Evil's Echo

Chapter One

THE DREAM SCENE STARRED twelve-year-old me diagramming a sentence on the blackboard in Sister Marie Madeline's seventh-grade English class at Merciful Heart. I was getting every word and phrase in exactly the right places when my jangling bedside phone interrupted. I juggled the receiver. "Hello."

"Butch, it's Harry. Did you pick up the call on your police band about the floater in the East River?"

I opened one eye. The bedside clock said 4:35. Did Harry really think I sat up all night listening to police calls? "Just a minute."

I threw back the covers, ran barefoot across the hardwood floor, and clicked on the radio. A tinny cop's voice. "Coast Guard spotted her snagged on some brush on the north side of Governor's Island."

Another voice. "What does it look like? A jumper?"

"They can't tell. They say no obvious COD."

I ran back to the phone. "I've got it on now."

The radio popped again. "They're bringing her in at the Coast Guard pier, next to the Staten Island Ferry building. Can you call the coroner to meet us there?"

Harry made a slurping sound, his wake-up coffee. "They say no obvious cause of death, so it's most likely a suicide. The story may wind up on the back page if Duke picks it up at all. Anyway, I'm going to hustle over there. Want me to swing by and pick you up?"

Harry Logan is a crime-beat reporter at the *New York Gazette* where I work. My stories carry the byline Eleanor Tracy, but the guys at the newspaper tagged me with my nickname, Butch, and the name stuck. They don't call me Butch because I'm a lesbian. I keep my private life pretty quiet around the office. They think they're being cute and ironic because of my size, five feet one and ninety pounds. Harry says someone started the nickname because

I'm spunky. If he means what I think he does, I choose to take it as a compliment.

I guess I developed my spunky personality early in life when my mother dropped me off on the doorstep of Sisters of the Merciful Heart in Wilmington, North Carolina with a note. "Passing through. Please take good care of Eleanor." One of the nuns added my last name Tracy because she was a fan of the comic strip detective Dick Tracy.

The sisters operate a combination orphanage and boarding school for girls. Sister Marie Madeline, our English teacher, was my angel. She paid special attention to me, gently combing the tangles out of the tight ringlets all over my head. When I cried for my mother and worried I had done something wrong to make her leave me, Sister Marie Madeline reassured me and dried my tears with a rough muslin handkerchief she kept tucked in her sleeve.

In English classes, she taught me to appreciate the orderliness of the rules of grammar and punctuation and to love reading books, especially mystery stories like Sherlock Holmes by Sir Arthur Conan Doyle and Mrs. Marple by Agatha Christie. When I graduated from Merciful Heart, I had read all the mysteries in our meager library, and I had my head set on a career as a newspaper crime reporter.

I got my job at the *Gazette* in 1967 about four years ago. I started as a copyboy, running stories from the reporters on the various beats, like police, city hall, and so on, to the editor in time for the next edition. Lots of reporters get a foot in the door as copyboys so I was excited to get the chance. I worked twice as hard as anyone else, and I got my shot at reporting, but not on the crime beat. I'm a society reporter. Duke Reynolds, my city editor, doesn't think a woman belongs out at all hours chasing robbers and murderers. Instead, I cover fancy weddings, debutante balls, and charity events. I also fill in for the lonely hearts columnist, "Dear Aunt Betty," when he's gone on a bender and disappears for a few days. Not my favorite assignments, but I figure they're a start. My buddy Harry, I guess you could call him my mentor, knows my ambitions so he tips me off when something promising comes along.

The radio crackled again. "I'm sending detectives and uniforms over from the Fifth. Don't let anyone touch anything till the coroner gets there."

"Right, boss."

Harry slurped his coffee again in my ear.

"Yeah, I'll wake up David and we'll meet you on the corner of Seventh and One Fourteenth." I glanced at the bedside clock. "Give us fifteen minutes."

I tested the shower temperature and stepped in, scrubbed the important parts, and stepped out. I brushed my teeth, gave my hair a desultory swipe with a pick, and threw on some slacks and a sweater. I added a blazer at the last minute and grabbed a peek in the mirror. It would do. I scooped up my bag, stumbled down the stairs, and banged on David and Gene's door.

David McAdams is the newspaper's staff photographer at the *Gazette.* He and his boyfriend Gene are my best friends and my landlords. My apartment is on the third floor of their brownstone on West 114th.

Gene answered my knock wearing a robe, boxer shorts, a T-shirt, and the dumb teddy bear slippers David gave him last Christmas. He had a book in one hand and a cup of coffee in the other.

"Good, you're awake." I grabbed the coffee and took a big swig.

He held up the book, *How To Pass The CPA Exam.* "Studying. David's sprawled across the bed snoring."

"Can you get him up? We're meeting Harry on the corner in seven minutes. They fished somebody out of the East River this morning."

"I thought you were supposed to be covering fancy parties. What are you doing up before dawn and headed to write a story about a dead person?"

"Just get David up. I'll grab his equipment. You ask too many questions."

Chapter Two

HERE'S HOW I CAME to New York and met David and Gene. Seven years ago, back in Wilmington when I finished twelfth grade at Merciful Heart, I enrolled in Dogwood State Junior College and got a job as a skating carhop at the Dairy Queen. I developed pretty good technique on the skates. I even performed a trick-skating show as a bonus for the customers. The entertainment upped my tips.

After two years of junior college, I had taken all the English and journalism classes the JC offered, and I had saved seven hundred and fifty dollars from my carhop job. I caught a Greyhound bus from Wilmington, North Carolina to Port Authority Bus Station in lower Manhattan to chase my dream of being a crime reporter.

I got a room at the Y with a communal bath down the hall and started making the rounds of Manhattan newspapers. No luck. No one was in the market for a five-foot, one-inch crime reporter with no experience. Since they don't have skating carhops in Manhattan, I got a job in the Columbia Journalism School cafeteria.

I spent days in a starched white uniform and a hairnet serving mashed potatoes and gravy to students. The only things that kept me going were the evening journalism classes I sneaked into in the massive lecture halls and regular letters from Sister Marie Madeline. Without that mental stimulation and Sister's affirmation and, I suppose, my spunky nature, I would have given up and gone back to Wilmington.

I haunted the Columbia housing office for leads on an apartment I could afford. Everything was too expensive. The office ladies got so used to seeing me that they just looked up and shook their heads when I walked in the door, indicating nothing new that fit my requirement: cheap.

A bulletin board hung outside the office. I hadn't paid much attention to the messages on the board before. Most of the postings advertised tutoring, yoga classes, or used textbooks. One beautifully hand-printed index card caught my eye. In big letters it said, "Outside the Box Rental." It offered a third-floor apartment in a brownstone on West 114th for fifty dollars a month with no details about what "outside the box" meant.

I copied the phone number and found a pay phone. A guy picked up after five or six rings. I heard the scream of a power saw in the background, and a deep, Southern-accented voice yelled, "Eugene! Turn that thing off a minute. Hello."

"I'm calling about your ad, the rental on a Hundred Fourteenth. I saw it on the bulletin board at Columbia."

"Right. Can you come over now?"

I ran all the way to the address he gave me, west of the park in the middle of the block. It was a brownstone with debris chutes running from windows on all three floors into a big blue dumpster parked next to the sidewalk. I checked the address twice. It was the right building. Sounds of hammering and sawing echoed into the street. A tall man in a yellow polo shirt moved past a window on the second floor. I knocked, but no answer. I backed up into the street. "Hey. Hello."

The guy in the yellow shirt stuck his head out the window. "Come on up. It's open. Second floor."

The smell of sawdust got stronger as I climbed to the second level. One room took up the whole floor, empty except for two sawhorses and a ladder. The man with the Southern voice on the phone said, "Hi, I'm David." He offered his hand. "And that's Gene." Gene pushed his safety goggles onto his forehead and waved.

"I'm Eleanor."

"You're interested in the apartment. Outside the box didn't put you off?"

"It's intriguing, I guess."

"You'll judge for yourself. Let's take a look at the place." He headed toward the stairs, and Gene put down the saw and followed us.

They must have started the renovations on the third floor because it was all finished. It was another big empty room painted white with refinished original hardwood floors. Windows overlooking 114th Street stretched across one side. Along the north side of the room, a small stove and refrigerator served as a neat little kitchen. David pointed to a walled-in corner. "That's the bathroom." I peeked in. There was a large shower and plenty of counter space. Everything looked brand new.

"What do you think?"

The apartment was much bigger and nicer than I'd expected. "Beautiful. Did you do this all yourselves? You two are very talented."

The one named Gene held up his hands. "That's David. I'm the hired help. I just do what I'm told."

I tried guessing the meaning of the outside-the-box part. There must be a catch. "The ad said fifty dollars a month."

Gene took three Budweisers out of the refrigerator. "We can use a break. Beer? The only place to sit is on the stairs."

"Thanks."

Gene passed me a bottle. "We'll waive the rent for the right person. We put the fifty bucks in to scare off weirdos. We're re-doing the bottom two floors for ourselves and this floor for a permanent rental. During construction, things will be loud at all kinds of hours and messy all the time. We can use an on-site caretaker until we're ready to move in. Rent will start then. We'll have to renegotiate at that time." He glanced at me sideways. "We're looking for the right person. Responsible and reliable."

"Sister Marie Madeline taught me to keep promises. She always said a person's only as good as his word."

David nudged me. "My grandma said the same thing. I can tell by your accent you're from the South. Where are you from, girl?"

"Wilmington, North Carolina."

David pointed at himself. "Greenwood, Mississippi."

Gene groaned. "Here we go. If this turns into a discussion about how the South is better, count me out. And I refuse to listen to another debate about who has the best bar-b-que."

David dismissed Gene with a wave. "Never mind him. He's from Pittsburgh. What brought you to New York?"

"I came to get a job as a reporter, but no luck so far. Right now I work at Columbia." It sounded better than saying I'm a lunch lady.

"It's a coincidence you want a reporter job. I'm a photographer at the *Gazette*. Maybe I can help. You'd have to be willing to start at the bottom of the ladder. The paper is always in the market for copyboys. You could work your way up. I'll happily introduce you to my buddy in personnel."

"That would be great."

Gene chugged the rest of his beer. "Give us a minute, Eleanor."

I went to the windows and watched a gaggle of kids in school uniforms, maybe third graders, follow their teacher along the sidewalk. They were paired up, two by two, holding each other's hands. I heard the power saw start again on the floor below.

David came and stood at the window with me. "The place is yours if you're interested."

"I'm very interested."

"If my grma were here, she'd say 'That makes us as happy as a pig in the peach orchard.'"

"Sister Marie Madeline would say, 'Bless your new home and those who visit you.'"

I moved my stuff from the Y the next day, and a week later I had a copyboy job at the *Gazette*. That was four years ago. David and Gene became the family I never had, and I got my heart's desire to be a reporter. Not exactly the kind of reporter I had in mind, but hope springs eternal.

Chapter Three

THE SUN WAS RISING over the Brooklyn skyline across the East River when David, Harry, and I spilled out of the taxi at the Coast Guard facility on the Manhattan side. Bands of blue, indigo, violet, and pink lit the horizon in the east. The Coast Guard boat, moored at the end of the concrete pier, bobbed on the swells kicked up by the Staten Island Ferry. Four uniforms and two plainclothes cops bent over a still form lying in a puddle of water. One of the detectives was a woman. Her dark hair was pulled back in a tight bun. Her perfectly bland gray suit and crisp white cotton blouse almost, but not quite, hid a killer figure. How did she manage to look that put together that early in the morning? I ran my hand down the front of my shirt, trying to smooth out some of the wrinkles.

David dug out his equipment and began popping flashbulbs. A dead person has a different stillness than a live one. More final. She wore a dress of lightweight floral fabric and her shoes were missing, lost in the river probably. I fought the urge to pull the skirt down to cover her thighs. She was young, her face smooth and unlined. Thick black hair fanned around her head. Her eyes were open and staring, the color so dark it was hard to tell where the pupil stopped and the iris started.

Dr. Harkness, the deputy coroner, brushed past me and shooed the cops away from the body. "Don't touch anything. I swear, it's like you guys have to learn over again with every case how to secure a crime scene." She took blue latex gloves from her black leather doctor bag, knelt beside the dead woman, and inspected her palms and the soles of her bare feet.

The male detective in the bunch of cops spoke. "What have you got? Anything on cause of death?"

Dr. Harkness didn't look up from her work. "Good morning, Detective Rollins."

Her tone would have withered a rose. I checked Rollins's face for some acknowledgment that he'd just been dissed, but he appeared clueless.

"Right, good morning, Dr. Harkness." He made a little bow. "Any signs how long she's been in the water?"

"From the wrinkling on her palms and the soles of her feet, given the river temperature, still warm this time of year, she's been in the water between twelve hours and three days. I can't be more precise until I get her back to the morgue. Ditto on the manner of death. If you want a working hypothesis, she went in the river from a height and died of concussion from the force of striking the water. Both legs appear broken and there's severe bruising around the ribcage. I suspect I'll find her organs ruptured when I open her up."

Rollins took out his little spiral notebook. "You say she went into the water from a height...do you mean jumped?"

"Or was pushed." Dr. Harkness stood up and motioned to two techs to zip the dead woman into a black body bag. "We'll have to see if the autopsy can shed any light on that."

He pointed toward the Brooklyn Bridge. "I suspect she took a swan dive off the bridge. We average a jumper every other month or so, and we're about due for one. Once you tell us how long she's been in the water, the boys in forensics can estimate where she went in according to the currents."

I rubbed my arms to smooth out the goose bumps. What would cause this young, beautiful woman to kill herself? You know how sometimes you just have an instinct about a thing? It's like an itch in your brain you can't scratch. I had a hunch this wasn't a suicide.

"Why hasn't she been reported missing?" Did I say that out loud?

Rollins pointed the eraser end of his pencil at me. "Who's this?"

Harry stepped between us. "She's with me. A fellow reporter at the *Gazette.*"

Rollins backed up a step. "What? Is Duke Reynolds sending schoolgirls out to crime scenes now?"

I was so surprised I couldn't think of a snappy comeback. I hate when that happens.

Harkness stripped off her gloves. "Don't be an ass, Rollins." She started packing her bag. "I'll call you after the postmortem, sometime this afternoon."

"Okay. In the meantime, I'll check the station. Maybe she's been reported missing." He said it just like that, as if I hadn't suggested it. Rollins turned to the woman detective who hadn't said a word the whole time. "You mop up here, Carr." He stuck his notebook in his coat pocket and headed for his car.

The woman detective directed the uniforms to search the Coast Guard boat and take the crew's statements.

Dr. Harkness dusted off the knees of her slacks. She nodded in Rollins's direction. "Don't waste your time worrying about Rollins. He doesn't like women. I should say, he doesn't like women who don't know their place, which he thinks is in the kitchen making his supper."

Harry took my arm. "Let's go. Nothing more to see here. Let's take the subway. It's faster this time of the morning. If I hustle, I can get something ready for the evening edition."

David began packing his gear. "I'll go with you and get these shots developed."

"You and David go ahead. I think I'll walk across the bridge and see what I can see."

Harry shrugged. "Suit yourself. I'm pretty sure Duke will deep-six the story. It appears to be a pretty straightforward jumper. Not much of interest to our readers." He glanced at the wet imprint the body left on the concrete pier. "Sad for the loved ones left behind, though."

The woman detective approached me and stuck out her hand. She shook with a firm grip. Not like some women who do the halfway limp finger shake. "Detective Christine Carr."

"Butch Tracy."

She leaned toward me. "Did you say Butch?"

"It's a nickname."

"I see." She nodded and smiled this fantastic smile that lit up her whole face.

"Obvious it's not my given name, I guess."

"Do you mind if I walk across the bridge with you? I'd like to see it for myself." A wisp of dark hair had escaped her bun, and she tucked the curl behind her ear.

"Don't mind a bit."

We headed north toward the pedestrian entrance to the bridge. Traffic was light that early in the morning. Detective Carr was taller than me with longer legs, and she was someone who kept in shape. She set a fast pace. I had to scurry to keep up.

The Brooklyn Bridge is supported by giant cables strung between two massive granite block towers, one close to the Manhattan side and one close to the Brooklyn side. We followed the plank walkway under the Manhattan tower. Its twin arched openings remind you of a Gothic cathedral, framing the Brooklyn skyline like stained glass windows. The arches don't serve any useful purpose. Maybe in 1883 when the bridge opened being practical wasn't so important.

It was mid-October, and the city was experiencing a spell of unseasonably warm weather. We stopped halfway across the bridge, between the granite towers, and looked south toward the Statue of Liberty and Governor's Island.

Detective Carr leaned over the railing. "The cables swag under the walkway here. If someone were going to jump, this would be the best place. You're less likely to bounce off something before hitting the water."

"Right." I couldn't help noticing how her slim skirt outlined a toned backside. The railing was not even waist high. For an anxious moment, I pictured her losing her balance and tumbling head over heels into the river.

She didn't, obviously.

The detective shielded her eyes. "Lady Liberty is still lifting her lamp beside a golden door, as the poem goes. If our Jane Doe went off the bridge at night, the landmark was the last thing she saw shining in the distance."

I looked around for where the dead woman might have left her shoes, which was a waste of time, of course. "Do you think she jumped?"

"I try to reserve judgment before all the facts are in."

"I know, but don't you ever get a gut feeling about something?"

"There are two kinds of people in the world, those who form a hypothesis and start gathering facts to support it, and those who collect the facts to form a complete picture before coming to a conclusion. I'm the second kind, and it's always served me well in my police work."

"Rollins seems to be jumping to the conclusion that Jane Doe committed suicide."

"Sometimes Rollins speaks before he thinks." Carr tucked the stray curl behind her ear again. "I'm glad for the opportunity to apologize for the way Rollins talked to you. He's not such a bad guy..."

"...Once you get to know him." We said it in unison.

"Yes, he's just kind of clueless."

"That is exactly the word that comes to mind."

"I'm new with NYPD, and they've assigned me to ride with him for part of my probationary period. We struggled for a few days, but he's coming around."

"Where were you before NYPD?"

"I transferred in from Buffalo PD."

"That must be a big change. What do you think of our city?"

"I've been too busy to see much of it." She pushed away from the railing. "Are you ready to start back? I need to get to the station."

"Yes."

Detective Carr started off at her speed-walking pace toward the Manhattan side. I struggled to both keep up and figure out a way to gracefully ask for her phone number.

We stopped on the street corner, and she stuck out her hand again. "Well, I'll grab a cab. Nice to meet you."

"Same here. Maybe I'll see you around."

"Maybe."

Chapter Four

OUR PAPER, THE *GAZETTE*, was founded in 1861, ten years after the *New York Times*. Over a hundred years later we are the older paper's major competitor for readership. We've always been considered the cheeky upstart. The *Times* fashions itself appealing to cultured, intellectual readers. They claim to report the news in a restrained and objective fashion, avoiding sensationalism. Their slogan is, "All the News That's Fit to Print." Implying, of course, the *Gazette's* readers are uncultured yahoos who want to read about scandals and gory murders. There may be something to that. Our city editor Duke Reynolds's slogan is, "If It Bleeds, It Leads."

I threw my bag in my chair and wound through the maze of reporters to Harry's desk. He was banging away on his typewriter and motioned me to have a seat. "Just let me finish this thought."

"Is that the Jane Doe in the East River story?"

"What? No. Duke nixed that. A mystery girl with no shoes or ID. Not enough answers. I've moved on to last night's shooting in Little Italy. Looks like a rival gang execution."

"What if I could get you more info about Jane Doe? Dr. Harkness promised Rollins autopsy results by this afternoon. Would Duke reconsider?"

"What about your own deadlines?"

"Dear Aunt Betty dried out, and he's back at work. David and I are covering a fancy party the mayor's hosting at Gracie Mansion tomorrow night, but I could work on your story till then."

"Great. If Duke runs it, I'll share the credit. Your first crime story byline."

"Thanks, Harry."

David walked up holding a stack of eight-by-ten glossies. "Thought y'all would like to see these shots from this mornin'." Every word out of David's mouth sounds like it's been dipped in honey. His Mississippi heritage.

"Harry's busy. I'll look them over." David and I wound our way back to my desk. "Harry said Duke passed on the story."

"You don't look happy about that."

"Detective Rollins is ready to write her off as a suicide. I'm not so sure." I picked up the pictures and began thumbing through them. "What if someone did this to her? Do they just get away with it?"

"What does the very attractive lady detective say? She's pretty, don't you think?"

"Yeah, but I probably won't see her again."

"Did you get her phone number?"

"I was working up to asking, but no."

He shook his head. "Darlin', you are hopeless. Anyway, what does she think about the dead woman?"

"That it's too soon to jump to conclusions."

He straightened the stack of photos on my desk. "This is an extra set, so you can keep them. Are you free for dinner? Gene's got a roast in the oven and you're invited."

"Not sure how late I'll be. I'm heading over to the coroner's to see what Dr. Harkness learned from the autopsy."

"See you later then." He sauntered off toward Duke's office, a glass cube in the middle of the newsroom. The editor was poring over copy for the evening edition. David stuck his head in and said something that made Duke laugh around the ugly cigar stub in his mouth.

I thumbed through the photos and stopped at a close-up of Jane Doe's face. Her expression was slightly surprised but oddly serene, like she was facing an assailant she knew and she was already forgiving him. I spun around in my chair to the desk behind mine. "Walt, got a minute?"

Walter Smith, the paper's most senior reporter, looked more like a college professor than a newspaperman. His reading glasses perched on the tip of his nose, and his thick gray hair curled over his shirt collar. He glanced up from a crossword puzzle he was working on with a fancy old-fashioned ink pen, the kind you actually put ink in. Where do you even buy ink nowadays? And how confident does a person have to be about their grasp of the English language to do the *Times* crossword in ink?

"Yes, Eleanor." Walt was the only guy in the newsroom who still used my given name.

"Hypothetically, how can a coroner tell if someone jumped off the Brooklyn Bridge or was pushed?"

"That is a very interesting question." He put down his pen and newspaper, folded his hands across his ample midsection, and leaned back in his chair.

I squirmed in my seat. I was in for a lecture with more information than I needed. When you ask Walt what time it is, get ready for an explanation of how a watch works.

"I assume in your hypothetical case there are no witnesses. As to the condition of the body, I suspect a pathologist would testify there is no difference between someone who was pushed and someone who jumped. The bridge is two hundred and twenty feet high. If the victim were alive when he hit the water, he would probably die of concussion, which is a sudden and violent explosion of the major organs and immediate catastrophic loss of blood. If he survived the drop, he would drown. In which case, there would be water in the lungs regardless of how he went off. Surprisingly, of the one thousand or so unfortunate souls who have jumped since the bridge opened, reportedly four have survived. The only explanation is divine intervention.

"But to your question, how to tell whether the victim jumped or was pushed. The pathologist would have to investigate the victim's state of mind in the time leading up to the event. Also, one would look for defensive wounds indicating a struggle before the fall."

"What signs of the victim's state of mind would you look for?"

"Feelings of hopelessness. Drop in performance at work or school. A major loss like the death of a loved one or the end of a relationship. Suicides usually show signs, though they may be subtle, of their desperation."

"Thanks, Walt. Very helpful. You're better than an encyclopedia."

"Happy to serve, my dear. You do raise an important point if your case is more than just hypothetical. Suicide is not a crime in the state of New York, and murder, of course, is."

Dr. Harkness had promised Detective Rollins some answers by the afternoon. I ran down the four flights to the street, grabbed a street vendor hotdog outside the *Gazette* building, and beat it back downtown.

The Chief Medical Examiner's office is in the five hundred block of First Avenue, across the street from Bellevue Hospital. I rode the elevator to the basement autopsy room. When the door slid open, I almost stumbled into a crying woman supported by a uniformed woman cop. "Excuse me." I stood aside and let them board the elevator. The crying woman looked a little older than me, maybe early thirties. She was blond and well-dressed.

A large window in one wall of the hallway lets the next of kin view a deceased without actually going into the autopsy room. Inside, Dr. Harkness, wearing a mask and blue scrubs, stood next to a metal autopsy table bearing a body covered with a sheet. She was making notes on a clipboard. I knocked on the window glass and waved.

She came to the door. "Hello, Butch. What can I do for you?"

"Any news on the Jane Doe?"

"Off the record, she's a Jane Doe no longer." She consulted her notes. "Dania Kapoor. Her friend was just here and ID'd the body."

That must have been the friend I almost tripped over at the elevator. I peeked around Harkness. "Okay if I come in?"

"Afraid not. I'll call Rollins to contact the next of kin. Can't have anything showing up in the paper before that."

"So I'll have to go through Rollins." I wasn't looking forward to putting up with his misogynistic BS.

She nodded. "Sorry."

"Were you able to determine how long she'd been in the water?"

"Thirty-six hours, give or take."

"How did they locate the friend? Background only. I won't quote you."

"She came into the police station to report Dania Kapoor missing. Rollins sent her over here to ID the body."

"Can you give me the friend's name?"

"Nope, but she had to sign that register hanging by the viewing window, and I'm too busy to talk any longer."

"Just one more question. Can you tell if Dania Kapoor jumped or was pushed?"

That was one question too many. She didn't respond. "Goodbye, Butch." The metal door swung shut in my face.

The register page had only one name on it: Sarah Quinn, 152 Hicks Street, Apartment C.

I took a cab to Hicks Street, a nice Brooklyn Heights residential area across the East River from lower Manhattan. I rang the bell for Apartment C. Another blonde, a little older than the woman I saw in the coroner's office and with shorter hair, answered the door. I handed her a card. "I'm a reporter from the *Gazette*. Is Sarah Quinn in?"

She stepped around the door and pulled it closed behind her. "How did you get this address?"

"Sarah reported a person missing. I'm trying to find information about that. Is she in?"

"I'm her sister, and she's not available. Please leave her alone." She stepped inside the door and moved to close it.

I stopped the door with my hand. "I'm just trying to find out what happened to Dania Kapoor."

"Ask her family."

"How can I locate them?"

"They own a market on Coney Island Avenue, Punjab Grocery. Leave Sarah alone." She slammed the door.

Chapter Five

CONEY ISLAND AVENUE IS the center of Little Pakistan, the largest concentration of Pakistani immigrants in the United States. Small businesses line the avenue on both sides, barber shops, travel agencies, cafés, markets, and clothing stores.

The sidewalks looked like pictures I had seen of open-air markets in Islamabad, all the merchandise piled outside the shops leaving hardly enough room for the shoppers. I stood across the street from Punjab Grocery sizing up the situation. Baskets of produce lined the front of the store. A green awning over the propped-open door advertised halal meats, fresh fruits and vegetables, and juice. Above the awning on the second floor, lace curtains framing open windows fluttered in the breeze. A woman in a headscarf leaned out the window and scanned the crowded sidewalk. A black Ford Fairlane stopped at the curb in front of the store and took my attention away from the woman. When I looked back, she was gone.

Detectives Rollins and Carr exited the Fairlane and went in the store. I jaywalked to the storefront, wedged myself between stacks of tomatoes and squash, and watched through the plate glass window. The space was crowded with women carrying mesh shopping bags. At the cash register, a young man in a spotless white cotton tunic and a dark beard counted a customer's change. A clerk stocked shelves behind him.

Rollins and Carr approached the man at the register and flashed their badges.

The man closed the cash drawer, spoke a few words to the clerk, and led the police to the back of the store and up some stairs.

A high, keening moan echoed from the apartment above. The detectives and the young man came into the street and drove away in Rollins's car.

I hailed a taxi and resisted the urge to say, "Follow that car." Rollins was in no hurry to get back to the station, and my cabbie was in a rush for his next fare, so we easily kept up with the Ford across the bridge into Manhattan. Rollins turned on Elizabeth Street and parked in a red zone in front of the 5th Precinct station house.

The building is the oldest still in use, completed in 1881. Once in a while, the city tries to close it and build a new modern station, but the ladies of the New-York Historical Society stage a protest, and the idea goes away till the next time. And, by the way, when you ask the ladies why there's a hyphen in the Society's title, they will tell you this is how the city spelled its name in 1804 when the group was founded, and that's good enough for them. I suspect it's an indication of their general attitude toward progress.

By the time I paid the cabbie and navigated the station's crowded waiting area, the detectives with the young man in the white tunic between them were headed up the wide staircase in the middle of the room. I glanced at the desk sergeant, perched behind his elevated desk with his nose in paperwork. Desk sergeants always look like they're busy with paperwork. I suspect they're avoiding dealing with the public. I started up the stairs.

The sergeant looked up. "Help you?"

I handed him my *Gazette* card. "I'm here to see Detective Rollins."

He picked up the phone, said a few words, then hung up. "He's busy."

"I'll wait."

"Suit yourself." He gestured toward the only seating, a long wooden bench like a church pew near the front door. It was fully occupied. I leaned against the wall to wait and watched the flow of humanity in and out of the front doors. A few people came in singles, pushing through the doors and pausing with dazed looks before approaching the desk sergeant. They came to report a crime or ask after a friend or relative. The larger number were handcuffed and led in by uniformed cops or detectives. They all had one thing in common: looks of misery and apprehension. No wonder the desk sergeant hid behind paperwork.

After half an hour, Rollins and the man in the white tunic came down the stairs. The detective shook hands and watched him head into the street.

I pushed away from the wall. "Detective Rollins. I'm Butch Tracy with the *Gazette*."

"Oh, yeah. You were with Harry Logan this morning."

"Right. What did you find out about Dania Kapoor?"

"I just spoke with her brother. It looks like a suicide."

"What did he say?"

"The family are devout Muslims. He and the sister had a disagreement, and she did the act that is prohibited by their religion and that would shame his family the most. She killed herself." He turned and started toward the stairs.

I stepped in his way.

"You're a spunky little package, aren't you?" That word again, spunky.

I didn't take the bait. "She killed herself over a disagreement?"

"It was more than that. Her brother was forcing her into an arranged marriage. Their father has died, and Amir is the head of the family now, and Dania was too much of a handful for him, poor guy. Appears to me he was looking to make her someone else's responsibility. Can't blame him for that. The night she died, she left in a huff with her suitcase."

Who packs a suitcase to commit suicide?

"Dr. Harkness says the body was in the water a day and a half before the cops found her. When she didn't come home, why didn't her brother report her missing?"

"He assumed she'd cool off and come back. She was only nineteen and had no place else to go."

"And what happened to the suitcase?"

"Listen, Miss Tracy. If you could see my desk, it's stacked with files on real murders, rapes, and burglaries. Suicide is not a crime. Stay out of my way and let me do my job." He stepped around me and up the stairs.

The next morning I went back to Brooklyn to try Sarah Quinn again. I rang the bell and stood up straight, preparing for the gatekeeper sister, but she had left. Sarah answered the door this time. Her eyes were rimmed with red.

I talked fast. "Miss Quinn, I don't mean to disturb you. Can I talk to you about Dania Kapoor?"

"The detectives have already been here." She started to close the door on me like her sister had.

"I'm not with the police. I'm a reporter. The police think Dania's death was a suicide. What do you think?"

She opened the door a little wider. "You said you're a reporter?"

"Yes, with the *Gazette*. I just want to write the truth, and I don't think the police are digging for the whole story. You must care about your friend. You did report her missing."

She hesitated. "I'm not sure how I can help. I have to get to work, so I have only a few minutes." She stepped aside to let me in and motioned toward a sofa. "I'm having my morning tea. Would you like a cup?"

"Thanks."

While she fixed my tea in the kitchen, I looked around the apartment. It was bigger than one you'd see in Manhattan, especially for a single person, but I didn't see any evidence of a spouse or roommate. Her taste was traditional, with chintz fabric upholstery and lots of prissy knickknacks scattered around. A pain in the neck to dust.

She brought the tea and set it on the coffee table.

"Thanks. May I call you Sarah?"

She nodded.

"You reported Dania Kapoor missing. What was your relationship with her?"

"When I first met her six months ago, I was her teacher, and we have become friends."

"You're a teacher?"

"I teach eighth-grade English at St. Ann's." She checked her watch. "A few months ago, I took a part-time adult school position teaching Business English at night." She looked around the apartment. "This neighborhood is nice but expensive. I needed the extra income. Dani was my student in the adult school class. She is very bright. She was special."

She clutched a wad of tissues that she picked at nervously as she talked. "We began spending time together. At first, we went for coffee after class then she began visiting me here." She sipped her tea. "She confided in me."

"Confided about what?"

"Her family are devout Muslins. They emigrated from Pakistan nine years ago, when Dani was ten years old. Dani grew up in Brooklyn in an American culture, and she and her father clashed. He was very domineering, and she has—had, a mind of her own."

"You say her father was domineering?"

"Yes. He passed away very unexpectedly about a year ago. Heart attack. It's just her mother and her brother Amir now. Dani and Amir were very close growing up. They are only a year apart in age. As they matured, the gender differences in their culture came between them. In Islam, the man is considered the protector of the family, and the woman makes a home for him and the rest. With the father gone, Amir is the head of the family and his and Dani's struggles have intensified. Dani disagreed with some of the decisions Amir made for her."

"Do you know the details of their disagreements?"

"She refused to wear traditional dress. She lived with her mother and brother and worked in their grocery store, but she dreamed of getting her education and finding a better job and a place of her own. Their religion doesn't exactly prohibit those things for women, but her father was very rigid, and now her brother is trying to enforce the same rules on his sister." Sarah dabbed at her eyes with the tissue. "Dania was very sensitive. She felt things very deeply."

"Did you know Amir was pushing Dania to agree to an arranged marriage?"

"Yes, it was the custom in Pakistan. She refused and Amir insisted. He expected Dania would go along with his position as head of the family, and as I said, Dani had a mind of her own."

"When is the last time you spoke with her?"

"She called three nights ago around nine o'clock and asked if she could come over. I said of course. I waited up till after one in the morning but she never came, and she wasn't in class the next night. I was concerned. She never missed class."

"When she called you, did she sound upset?"

"No, in fact just the opposite. She sounded especially upbeat. When she didn't show up for class, I called the number Dani had given me but didn't get an answer. That's when I went to the police."

Walt said people thinking about suicide show signs. "Have you noticed any drop in the quality of her schoolwork?"

"Oh, no. Dani is by far my best pupil."

"She hasn't seemed hopeless?"

"Hopeless? No, she was a very positive person."

"You said the police were here?"

"Yes. Just a minute." She left the room and came back with two business cards belonging to Detective Rollins and Detective Carr. She dropped them in front of me on the coffee table.

"And you told them what you just told me?"

"Yes."

"Sarah, is it possible Dania Kapoor could have committed suicide?"

She pushed up from the chair. "Excuse me." She ran to another part of the apartment, I guessed to a bedroom or bathroom. I heard quiet sobs. After a few minutes, she came back. "I'm sorry. You have to go now."

I put my *Gazette* business card on the coffee table next to Rollins's. "Please call me if you can shed any more light on what happened to Dania or if you just want to talk."

On my way back to the paper, I stopped by the coroner's office to see if Harkness would give me any more details for Harry. Curtains blocked the view into the autopsy room, so I figured

Harkness was busy in the middle of an examination. I turned back to the elevator as she came hustling out of the swinging doors with her black bag.

"Dr. Harkness. I know Dania Kapoor's family has been notified, so can you spare a minute about what you learned in the autopsy?"

"You can walk with me, but I'm on a call for a pileup in the Lincoln Tunnel. Make it fast."

I pulled out my notebook. "Dania's cause of death?"

"There's a distinction between manner of death and cause of death. Manner of death in this case was concussion with numerous burst internal organs and catastrophic internal bleeding. No signs of a struggle. No defensive wounds. Water in the lungs, so she survived long enough to take a few last breaths." On the curb, Harkness stuck her hand up for a cab. "Cause of death is trickier. There are officially six possibles in New York State: natural, accidental, suicide, homicide, undetermined, and pending. I detest the prospect of having to rule a death undetermined or pending. I believe we owe the loved ones an answer. Therefore, I'm not ready to make a ruling yet."

A cab pulled to a stop, and she jumped in. They were off before I could say thanks.

Chapter Six

THE NEWSROOM WAS BUZZING with activity. Copyboys ran back and forth between reporters and Duke's in-basket. The air smelled of cigarette smoke and felt close and heavy. The air circulation system in the old *Gazette* building never seemed quite up to the challenge of all those bodies jammed together. I waved across the room at Harry and got busy. I scrolled a sheet of paper into my typewriter and began notes for Harry on what I'd learned so far.

The deceased was Dania Kapoor, 1026 Coney Island Boulevard, Brooklyn. Lived with her mother and brother. Worked in the family grocery and part-time student. Approximately 36 hours in the water before the Coast Guard spotted her.

Reported missing yesterday morning by Sarah Quinn, 152 Hicks Street, Apartment C, Brooklyn. Quinn ID'd the body too. Quinn was a teacher and friend. She spoke on the phone with Dania around 9:00 three nights ago. The family didn't report Dania missing. Rollins brought the brother in this morning. He said he and Dania had an argument and the family assumed she left home because of it. They didn't report her missing because they expected her to get over it and come home.

Rollins is convinced the death is a suicide. Harkness says she died of "concussion," meaning her organs all exploded from the force of the fall. She found no defensive wounds. She isn't ready to report a cause of death, whether Dania jumped or was pushed.

I found Harry in the coffee room. He skimmed the notes and folded the paper and put it in his pocket. "This is great, Butch. I'll wait till there's a cause of death to have another go at Duke with the story. If she got pushed, he'll let us chase the story. We don't want to get blown off again, right?"

I headed back to my desk and almost collided with Walt Smith coming out of the men's room. "Sorry, Walt. I need to pay attention to where I'm going."

"Distracted by your hypothetical suicide?"

"Something like that." The phone on my desk jangled. "Tracy."

"Miss Tracy, this is Sarah Quinn. You left your number and said I could call you. Can I speak to you again about Dani Kapoor?"

"Yes."

"Not over the phone. Can you possibly come back to my apartment?"

"I'll be there in fifteen minutes."

I was there in twelve minutes. The dead bolt clicked, and she opened the door. Her face was ashen, and her eyes were even redder.

She collapsed on the sofa. "I'm responsible for Dani's death."

I sat next to her. "What do you mean?"

"I don't know why I'm telling you this. You're a newspaper reporter. I just don't have anybody to talk to. I suppose I thought you might be...sympathetic. Will you be? I don't think I can live with lying about Dani. I couldn't bear to go to school today. I had to call in sick."

"Go on."

"I lied to the police and to you. Dani wasn't just dropping by my apartment that night as I implied. She was set on moving in with me. She called to say she had her bag packed, and she was coming. She sounded so excited and happy."

Sarah looked up at me with a plea in her eyes. "I don't know how to explain to you why I let things get that far. I should have put a stop to her crush when I recognized it. I knew it, of course. That's happened often enough in my career. I suppose I felt flattered. She was so attractive and smart and optimistic. Dani believed anything is possible here in America. I didn't resist her when things went beyond just flirting, and once we got started, I was in too deep."

She clutched my sleeve. "She wasn't a child. She was nineteen."

"When she called, did she mention an argument with her brother?"

"Yes, the struggle between Dani and Amir over the arranged marriage was coming to a head. For several weeks, she's been hinting about moving in with me. I counseled her to give it some time. I worried about her defiance. I knew she would pay a heavy price for resisting the family's wishes, and I didn't want to be responsible for that."

She ran her fingers through her hair and shook her head. "That's not the whole truth either. I wasn't ready to take such a big step with Dani. She was so young, and I was terrified of being found out and losing my job. That night on the phone I should have told her not to come, but I wanted to let her down easy in person."

I tried to imagine how Sarah would let a bright, sensitive nineteen-year-old down easy. "And she showed up?"

"Yes, just as she said, with her suitcase."

"Did you tell her she couldn't move in?"

"I didn't get a chance. I was making some hot chocolate for us when Amir banged on the front door. He was angry. Beyond angry, enraged. He made terrible accusations and threatened to report me to St. Ann's. He demanded that Dani go with him, and she agreed, I think to try and calm him down. When she didn't come back, I knew something awful had happened, but I never dreamed..." She dropped her head in her hands and sobbed.

I waited till she quieted. "I guess you didn't tell Detectives Rollins and Carr any of this."

She pushed up from the sofa and began pacing. "I should have told the detectives the truth about that night, but you must understand. If my school finds out about Dani and me, I'll not only lose my position at St. Ann's, but I'll never be allowed in a classroom anywhere." She grabbed my sleeve again. "What should I do? I have to tell Detective Rollins, don't I?"

I picked up Detective Carr's card. "Where's your phone?"

The receptionist at the police station put me through to Carr. "Detective, I hope you remember me. Butch Tracy, from the *Gazette*."

"Of course. What can I do for you?"

"It's about the Dania Kapoor case."

"I'm afraid I can't talk to the press, Butch. That's above my pay grade."

"I'm not calling as a reporter right now. I'm with Sarah Quinn, the woman who reported Dania missing and identified her body. Sarah has some important information about the night Dania died. Can you come talk to her? I think it's best done in person."

"Yes, I can be there in half an hour."

"And can you come alone?"

I was relieved she didn't ask why.

Carr got there in fifteen minutes. Sarah repeated her story about the last time she saw Dania. Detective Carr asked penetrating questions, including about the nature of Sarah and Dania's relationship. Asking Carr to come was a good call. Sarah haltingly disclosed the whole truth.

Carr looked up from her notes. "What time did Dania leave with Amir?"

"About ten o'clock."

"Where is the suitcase? Did Dania leave it when she went with Amir?"

Sarah went into the bedroom and came back with a scuffed brown valise. Carr pulled latex gloves from her pocket and popped the latches. Inside were what must have been all of Dania's belongings. Sarah hiccuped a sob.

"Do you recognize these clothes as being Dania's?"

Sarah nodded.

Carr stood up. "We'll be in touch, Miss Quinn. We'll need you to come to the station and sign a statement."

Sarah nodded again.

I followed the detective to the street. "Are you going to talk to Amir?"

"Headed there now."

"Can I go along?"

"We're still off the record?"

"Yes."

"Then you can come."

The market had a closed sign in the front window, but Amir was at the register counting receipts. Carr knocked on the glass. He came to the door. "The market is closed."

Carr showed her badge. "Detective Carr. We spoke the other day about your sister's death. Can we come in?"

"I told you and the other detective all I know. My mother and I are in mourning. We would appreciate some respect for our loss."

"I have a few questions about your sister and Sarah Quinn. I prefer to talk inside." She glanced over her shoulder. "Away from the street."

When Carr said Sarah Quinn's name, Amir's lips narrowed to a thin straight line. He moved away from blocking the door to let us pass and went back around the counter. He slammed the cash drawer shut so hard the machine rang.

Carr consulted her notes. "You told Detective Rollins and me the last time you saw Dania was in her bedroom in your family's apartment upstairs at about nine o'clock the night of her disappearance. You said she packed a suitcase and left without telling you or your mother where she was going."

"That's right."

"Were you at Sarah Quinn's apartment at about ten o'clock that night?"

Amir's nostrils flared, and he pounded his fist on the counter. "You're here harassing us when you should be arresting that woman. She took advantage of my sister, and she's the cause of Dania's death." He reached under the counter and came up with a pistol pointed at Carr's chest.

"Stop, Amir!" His head jerked toward the shout.

A woman dressed in a black ankle-length skirt and long-sleeved high-necked blouse stood in the doorway at the back of the store. A black headscarf covered her hair.

"Go back upstairs, Mother."

"You have to tell them the truth, Amir."

"Do you want me to go to prison? What will you do then? I told you it was an accident, but do you think they'll believe me? We're not white Christians. There'll be no justice for us."

Carr pulled me behind her. "Mr. Kapoor, put the gun down. You'll only make matters worse."

"Go with them, son. I'll call the Imam. He'll know what to do."

All the air went out of Amir. He seemed to consider his options for a few beats, then laid the pistol on the counter and dropped his head in his hands. "They'll never believe me."

Carr took a giant step and snatched up the pistol. "Hands on your head and walk slowly backward toward me." Carr cuffed his hands behind his back. "Amir Kapoor, I'm arresting you for threatening a police officer with a gun. You have the right to remain silent. Anything you say can and will be used against you in a court of law. You have a right to an attorney. If you can't afford an attorney, one will be provided for you. Do you understand?"

He nodded. "Call Imam Furquan, Mother."

The detective led Amir to the car and tucked him in the back seat. "Here's where we part ways, Butch. I have to get him back to the station."

"What happens next?"

"He'll be booked for the threatening a police officer charge. Dr. Harkness notified us she's calling a coroner's inquest in ten days to determine the cause of Dania's death. We'll have to see what happens after that."

Chapter Seven

HARRY AND I JOINED a dozen or so people milling around the front door of the first-floor hearing room in the medical examiner's headquarters. Mrs. Kapoor, Dania and Amir's mother, sat on a bench between two men in white tunics. She held herself perfectly straight and still, her face betraying no emotion.

"That's Amir and Dania's mother on the bench, but who are the rest of these people, Harry?"

"A coroner's inquest is public. This group makes a hobby of attending these things. What the attraction is, don't ask me. I suppose it's like watching the Perry Mason show in person. They're hoping for a dramatic courtroom confession moment."

At precisely nine o'clock, a clerk opened the doors and we trouped in. The space looked like a cross between a conference room and a judge's courtroom. There was no raised bench at the front, just a regular table with seating for Dr. Harkness, the clerk, and a stenographer, and a witness chair to the right. Two tables faced the coroner's spot. The rest of us took seats in the audience.

A woman down the row from Harry and me pulled her knitting out of her bag. A side door opened and Detectives Rollins and Carr led Amir and his attorney to one of the front tables, and they took the other. The attorney put his arm around Amir's shoulders. We couldn't see Amir's face, but his head was bowed, and the attorney whispered in his ear every so often and patted his arm.

Dr. Harkness and a stenographer came in a side door across the room and took their seats. There was no "all rise" like in a courtroom.

Harkness opened a file. "By the authority vested in me by the state of New York, I am convening a hearing to determine the official cause of death of Dania Kapoor, accidental, suicide, or homicide.

"Miss Kapoor's remains were recovered from the East River. I have conducted a postmortem examination of the deceased, and my report will be appended to the transcript of this hearing. I found the manner of death to be concussion and consequent sudden and catastrophic internal blood loss. My examination showed no external wounds with no evidence of a struggle. This hearing will focus on Miss Kapoor's state of mind at the time of her death and the testimony will be limited to that topic. NYPD is currently investigating the circumstances surrounding Miss Kapoor's death, and that part of the case I will leave up to them."

She turned to the clerk. "Swear in Detective Claude Rollins, NYPD."

Rollins stood and took the oath.

"State your name."

"Detective Claude Rollins."

"Have a seat, Detective. How long have you been with the New York Police Department?"

"Twelve years."

"And when did you attain the rank of detective?"

"Five years ago."

"And what territory are you assigned to?"

"I'm out of the Fifth Precinct."

"How long have you reported to the Fifth?"

"All five years after my promotion."

"Did you receive a call in the early hours of October twelfth to investigate a body recovered from the East River?"

"I did. My partner, Detective Carr, and I responded."

"Was the body recovered in the jurisdiction of the Fifth Precinct?"

"No, it was in the First."

"Why were you and Detective Carr dispatched?"

"It appeared she jumped off the Brooklyn Bridge, which is located in the Fifth, so my captain called us."

"You say it appeared she jumped from the bridge. So you assumed Dania Kapoor was a suicide?"

"Well, yes. We get five or six of these cases a year, and this one looked like another one of those. That's why the captain dispatched Carr and me to the scene."

"So you and Detective Carr set about investigating the case. Walk me through that."

"Well, first we had to establish the deceased's identity. There was no ID on the body. I checked missing persons and established Miss Kapoor's friend, Sarah Quinn, had reported her missing. I sent Miss Quinn with a uniformed officer here to your autopsy room to ID the body, and she did so."

"What did you do then?"

"Detective Carr and I went to notify the next of kin, her mother and brother, Amir Kapoor." He nodded toward Amir. "We brought Mr. Kapoor into the station, and he told us he and his sister argued, and she packed her bag and left the home. He assumed she would cool off and return since she had no other place to go. That's why they didn't report her missing."

"Mr. Kapoor stated his sister left with a suitcase."

"That's right."

"Did it seem odd that Miss Kapoor would pack a suitcase before committing suicide?"

"People do strange things."

"Did you subsequently locate the suitcase?"

"My partner, Detective Carr, located it."

"We'll hear from Detective Carr about that. What is the status of the Dania Kapoor investigation now?"

"It's pending the results of this hearing."

"Thank you, Detective. Call Detective Christine Carr."

The clerk swore Detective Carr in.

"State your name for the record."

"Detective Christine Carr."

"How long have you been with NYPD?"

"Three months."

"What territory are you assigned to?"

"I'm serving a probationary period of six months. I'm finishing up with the Fifth Precinct this week and tomorrow headed over to the Ninth to complete my probation."

"You started with NYPD as a detective?"

"Yes, I transferred here from Buffalo PD."

"How long did you serve at Buffalo PD?"

"Twelve years."

"And what was your rank there."

"I was a captain."

"But you are still required to serve a probationary period for a line detective position with the New York police?"

"Yes, it's standard policy. I have to learn the ins and outs of the city and the agency. Buffalo is a much smaller department, of course."

"Did you work murder cases in Buffalo?"

"Yes, as a line detective I was in major crimes, which involved investigating murders. As a captain, I was in charge of a geographic area in a high-crime part of the city, so unfortunately there were many instances of murder."

"Does your experience include investigating suicides?"

"Yes, I have investigated suicides."

"On the morning of October twelfth, you responded to the discovery of Miss Kapoor's body with your partner, Detective Rollins, correct?"

"That's correct."

"Detective Rollins testified he suspected the victim was a suicide. Did you agree?"

"We were just beginning the investigation, so I hadn't come to any conclusion yet."

"Detective Rollins testified you recovered Miss Kapoor's suitcase after her death."

"That's right. Miss Kapoor left the suitcase at Sarah Quinn's apartment in Brooklyn. She's the woman who reported Miss Kapoor missing and who identified the body. Miss Quinn recognized the contents of the case as Miss Kapoor's belongings."

"Did you find it unusual that a person contemplating suicide would go to the trouble of packing a bag?"

"In my experience, yes, that would be highly unusual."

"Thank you, Detective. Call Dr. Carl Roper."

The clerk left the room and came back with a tall thin man in a tweed jacket with leather patches on the elbows and horn-rimmed glasses. The clerk swore him in, and he took the chair next to Harkness.

"State your name and title for the record."

"Carl W. Roper, PhD."

"What is your profession, Dr. Roper?"

"I'm a forensic psychologist and a professor of psychology in the graduate school at New York University."

"And for the record, what is a forensic psychologist?"

"We apply psychological knowledge and methods to help answer legal questions arising in civil, criminal, contractual, or administrative proceedings, such as this inquest."

"You have authored several scholarly articles on the causes of suicide in young people, is that correct?"

"Yes, and several textbooks on suicide in general."

"Would you call yourself an expert on the psychological aspects of suicide, Dr. Roper?"

"That might be presumptuous, but other people have noted my particular expertise. I have testified at over a hundred similar trials and inquests."

"And we have retained you to help determine Dania Kapoor's state of mind before her death."

"That's right."

"Do you have an opinion today about the victim's state of mind and how it might relate to her cause of death?"

"I do."

"What method did you employ to inform your opinion?"

"I interviewed the deceased's mother, her brother, two of her classmates, and her teacher."

"In your research, what are the common signs that a young person is contemplating suicide?"

"Victims of suicide generally display several signs of an impending event. These can often be subtle, but in our research they are remarkable in their commonality. There is a feeling of hopelessness, helplessness, and worthlessness. They demonstrate a drop in performance at work or at school."

I whispered to Harry, "That's exactly what Walt Smith said, my own personal encyclopedia."

"They avoid being around other people and experience changes in eating and sleeping patterns. They lose interest in normally enjoyable activities."

"Did any of the friends and family report these behaviors in Dania Kapoor?"

"No, on the contrary, she was generally an upbeat, positive person, and she had seemed to be particularly cheerful and optimistic recently. She had plans for the future. She was an excellent student, dedicated to her studies."

"You stated you have an opinion about whether Dania Kapoor committed suicide. What is your opinion?"

"In my opinion, Miss Kapoor did not commit suicide."

The crowd in the room buzzed. Amir's lawyer leaned in to whisper in his ear.

Dr. Harkness spoke to her clerk and looked around the auditorium. "I've asked my clerk to remove anyone from the room who disturbs these proceedings in any way. If you wish to remain in the room, please stay silent. Thank you, Dr. Roper. Call Amir Kapoor."

Amir and his attorney stood up.

Harry and I scooted a little closer to the edge of our seats. The set of Amir's shoulders squared, and he stood taller.

"Mr. Kapoor, I understand your religion forbids swearing in court, so I will ask you to affirm that you will answer my questions truthfully. You are bound by the same laws whether you swear or not. Do you understand?"

He answered in a clear voice. "Yes."

"Thank you. Have a seat. How old are you, Mr. Kapoor?"

"Twenty years old."

"How old were you and your sister when your family came to America?"

"I was ten and my sister was nine years old."

"Why did your family immigrate to this country from Pakistan?"

"There was a coup d'état, and many violent demonstrations in the streets, and my father was afraid for our safety. He was the private physician to the deposed president, so he felt he had a target on his back and therefore his family was in danger."

"Was your father a physician here in the US?"

"No. We own a market in Brooklyn."

"You and your sister were only a year apart in age?"

"Yes."

"Can you describe your relationship with her?"

"When we were young, we were very close. We spoke no English at first, and my parents couldn't afford private school. We left our country in the dark of night with only the clothes on our backs and what few possessions we could carry. Dania and I went to public grade school and junior high in Brooklyn. We supported each other and helped with schoolwork and learning English. We were best friends."

"So you and your sister graduated from public high school?"

"When I was fifteen, I changed to the mosque school. Dania refused to change, so she stayed in the public high school."

Harkness checked her notes. "Your father passed away a year ago when you were nineteen. Is that right?"

"Yes."

"You became head of your household?"

"Yes."

"Would you say you and your sister were close during the past year?"

Amir hesitated. "We were family."

"Were you with your sister on the evening of October ninth?"

"Yes."

"You told the detectives you and Dania argued that night. She left the apartment with a suitcase, and you did not see her alive after she left. Is that your testimony this morning?"

"No, Your Honor."

"I'm not Your Honor. Dr. Harkness will do." She shuffled some papers in the file. "Just so our record is clear, I'm about to ask you to describe the events of October ninth, and your testimony will differ from what you initially told the police?"

"Yes."

"Why did you lie to the police, Mr. Kapoor?"

"I was afraid I would not be believed, and the police would send me to jail. With Dania dead, I'm all my mother has now."

From behind, Mrs. Kapoor showed no reaction. She sat poker straight between the two men who came with her.

"Tell me about that evening."

"We closed the market around six as usual. We had a dinner guest that night, Mr. Patel. Before dessert, Dania abruptly excused herself from the table and disappeared into her bedroom. Mr. Patel had come to dinner specifically to spend time with Dania. Her behavior was very rude. She embarrassed my mother and me. After Mr. Patel left, I went to her bedroom to discuss it with her and found her packing a suitcase. We argued. She stormed out of the apartment."

"Did she tell you where she was going?"

"To her teacher's apartment in Brooklyn Heights, Miss Quinn."

"What happened next?"

"My mother was very upset and asked me to go to Miss Quinn's apartment and convince my sister to come home. I went there, but Dania refused to return to our home with me."

"What did you do?"

"I refused to leave without her."

"Did you put your hands on her at that time?"

"No."

"What next?"

"She agreed to go outside and discuss the situation privately. We walked to the bridge and followed the plank walkway toward Manhattan. Halfway across, she turned and began to run back toward the Brooklyn side. I caught up with her."

"Did you put your hands on her at that time?"

"Yes, I was trying to make her stop and listen."

"What next?"

"We struggled. She lost her balance."

Everyone in the room held their breath. Street noise drifted in an open window.

"She went over the railing. For a split second, I had her hand, but she slipped out of my grasp."

A soft sob from Mrs. Kapoor broke the silence. Amir turned and looked at his mother with the most sorrowful expression I have ever seen on a human being's face.

"Do you need a break, Mr. Kapoor?"

He shook his head. He wanted to get it over with.

"I went home and told Mother, and we went to the mosque. The Imam prayed with us. He told us we must put it in Allah's hands, and that's what we have done."

"Thank you, Mr. Kapoor. Call Imam Furquan."

The clerk escorted a bearded man in the traditional white tunic into the room and indicated the seat next to Dr. Harkness.

"Imam, do you affirm that you will tell this inquest the truth?"

"I do."

"State your name and your position at Masjid Al Islam in Brooklyn?"

"Imam Jakob Furquan. I lead the community in common prayer."

"Do members of the community also seek your advice during tragic and stressful times in their lives?"

"Yes."

"The Kapoor family are members of your community?"

"Yes. The father was a leader in our community before his death, and his son, Amir, is following in his footsteps."

"Did Mrs. Kapoor and her son Amir come to the mosque on the night of October ninth?"

"They did."

"Tell me what happened."

"They came at about midnight. Amir described the terrible accident that had just occurred involving his sister on the bridge. We prayed and read together the prophet's words. Mrs. Kapoor and Amir stayed for about two hours."

"Were they comforted?"

"They appeared so. Islam teaches us not to fear death and to embrace our fate in the next world. While it is easy to fear the pain of death or the unknown, it is in fact our lives here on earth today that we must fear the most. For those who truly believe in Allah, death is a welcome passage."

"Did you sense that Amir told you the truth about the circumstances of his sister's death?"

"Yes."

"Thank you, Imam."

Harkness gathered her papers and closed the file. "Given the results from my postmortem examination and the evidence presented at this inquest today regarding the deceased's state of mind, I find the cause of Dania Kapoor's death to be accidental. The coroner's report will so state. Thank you all."

Harry grabbed Rollins for a statement and I pulled Detective Carr aside. "What about your investigation of Dania's death? Does it mean Amir won't be charged?"

"Looks like it. The DA isn't likely to go against a coroner's finding of accidental death."

"So Sarah Quinn's secret will stay a secret. She'll keep her job."

"Yep."

"What about the charge of pulling a gun on us? Will they stick Amir with that?"

"Not if I have anything to say about it. I'll recommend they let him plead it down to obstructing an officer and give him probation. Amir's right about his mother needing him now more than ever."

I started to ask for her phone number. It wasn't the best time, but you have to take your opportunities where you find them. "Well…"

Rollins interrupted. "Let's go, Carr. We have to get him back to jail."

"Right. See you around, Butch."

"I hope so."

The next morning, Duke Reynolds gave me the news that Dear Aunt Betty had disappeared again. I was just finishing the advice column when Harry slapped the morning *Gazette* on my desk. "Have you seen the Kapoor story? Your first crime byline."

"Yeah, I saw it. Page sixteen."

"It's not front page above the fold, but you've got to start somewhere."

"Thanks for letting me come along for the ride, Harry."

"I'd say you were more than along for the ride. Duke was complimentary, and he's a hard man to impress. You cracked the case for Rollins. Wonder what the detective thinks of women reporters now?"

"I won't hold my breath for a dramatic change."

Chapter Eight

HARRY RUSHED PAST MY desk, struggling to get his arms through the sleeves of his overcoat. He pushed the elevator button and as an afterthought yelled across the room at me. "Get your coat, Butch. We've got another death. This time it's in midtown."

We rode down to the first floor. "David's going to meet us there with his equipment. A buddy of mine at the Criminal Courts building called me with the tip. It's somebody important."

"Will the police let us in?"

"If we're lucky, Detective Sloane caught the case. He owes me a favor."

The cab let us off in front of the imposing hall of justice. A uniformed cop stopped us at the door. "Building's closed today."

We showed our press IDs, and he pointed us toward the elevators. "Judge Hawthorne's chambers on the third floor."

Harry winked at me. "So far, so good."

The judge's chambers was at the end of a deserted marble hallway. Inside the heavy oak door, a draft blowing in large open windows billowed a hanging figure's black robe. My second dead body in the space of two weeks. A thick rope, tied to a 1940s' ceiling fan, ended in a noose around the neck of the lifeless figure. The judge's face was livid. His eyes bulged in their sockets, and his black tongue lolled out of his mouth. The body rotated in a lazy circle, and the fan groaned with each rotation. It was a gruesome pirouette.

In the corner, Detective Mike Sloane talked quietly with a woman crying into a handkerchief. He looked up when we came in the door, then gave Harry a little wave.

Harry whispered behind his hand. "We're in luck. You'd better stand back a little. We need to stay out of his way." He motioned toward the corner with his pencil. "Stand over there, Butch."

I watched the body make another turn. "Can't someone shut off the fan? It's kind of disrespectful, don't you think?"

"It's off. The wind in his robe is making him turn. Harkness will show up soon to take him down."

A wooden straight chair lay tipped over under the body, and a forensics tech was dusting it for prints. The corpse made another slow turn. His hands were tied behind his back. No way the cops could jump to the conclusion this was a suicide as Rollins had with Dania Kapoor. I pictured the judge with a noose around his neck balancing on the tiptoes of his highly polished Florsheims and a hand shoving the chair over. How had the killer managed to get him to climb up there?

Wait. Detective Sloane covers murders in the Ninth Precinct. That's where Detective Carr said she would be assigned for the rest of her probation. Just as I finished the thought, Carr walked in the door balancing a paper cup full of water for the witness. She looked great, as always. She gave me a tiny wave and a nod. I felt a little buzz in my solar plexus.

The witness drained the water and wiped her nose and took a deep breath. "I came in early. I always come in early before anyone else to get a start on organizing the day's calendar. Judge Hawthorne insists on everything being organized." She looked up at the body. "And there he was, just hanging there."

"When did you last see Judge Hawthorne alive?"

"When I left yesterday. Our last case finished at four thirty. He told me he had some reading to catch up on. I left at about five. He was planning to attend an Inns of Court board meeting at six thirty. That's a professional organization. The judge was very active in the group. He was a leader." That sent her off on another crying jag.

David came in, unloaded his equipment, and started taking pictures. I tugged on David's sleeve. "Get a close-up shot of the note on the front of the judge's robe."

"Yep." A flashbulb popped and lit up the paper. I inched forward to get a better look. The killer had thumbtacked the note to the victim's chest. Cold-blooded. He could have used tape or a paperclip. Printed in red block letters, the note said THE SINS OF THE FATHER ARE TO BE LAID UPON THE CHILDREN. At the bottom was a symbol, a circle with a cross in the middle, like looking through a rifle scope.

Dr. Harkness arrived and began walking around the body taking notes. Sloane left the witness with Carr and approached the coroner. "What have we got, Dr. Harkness?"

"Likely not a suicide with his hands tied behind his back. That's one good thing. Chances are we won't need an inquest to establish this one's a homicide. Judging by the lividity, he's been dead since about seven p.m. last night. Manner of death either broken neck or strangulation. Hard to tell for sure until we get him back to the morgue for a postmortem. For his sake, I hope it was a broken neck. The other is a very hard way to go. We'll run a toxicology screen to see if there was anything more than the hanging. No other obvious trauma and no defensive wounds visible."

Sloane scratched his head with his pencil. "That's odd. The judge just climbed on the chair and let the guy put a rope around his neck?"

That was my question exactly.

Dr. Harkness shrugged. "The answer to that one's your department, not mine." She motioned to two assistants. One held the corpse by the legs to release the tension while the other untied the rope. They lowered the body onto a gurney, draped a sheet over him, and wheeled him toward the door. The edge of his black robe stuck out below the sheet.

Sloane arranged for the crying witness to come to the station in the afternoon to give a written statement. "Show her out, Carr, and check with that Inns of Court outfit to see if the judge showed up at the meeting." Detective Carr waited while the witness gathered up her things and led her out the door with her arm around her shoulders. Harry took the opening to approach Detective Sloane.

"What do you make of this so far?"

"Off the record?"

"Yeah, background only."

"It's pretty obvious retribution for some sentence the judge handed down. The building's open, so anybody could have come in off the street. We'll check the judge's past trial calendars against the names of scumbags who have recently been released from prison, starting with Attica. My bet is we'll find the killer on that list."

I jumped in. "What about the note? What about 'the sins of the father'?"

Sloane made a face. He looked like he wanted to spit. "Who knows what's in the minds of these vermin? Sounds like to me the killer is just juicing up the story so he can get more attention from people like you and Harry."

I watched Harry's expression for some reaction, but his face showed nothing. He looked to be buying the detective's theory that the murderer was looking for payback on the judge.

I wasn't so sure the motive for this murder was as straightforward as Sloane and Harry thought.

David started packing up his equipment. He motioned me over. "I've got all I need here, and you and I are due at the Waldorf tonight for the Met Gala. I have to go by the paper to get these photos processed, then by the apartment and change into my tux." He eyed my rumpled khaki slacks. "Are you going to wear your little black number again?"

"Yeah. You go ahead home. It takes you longer to get ready than me anyway. I'll meet you at the coffee shop across the street from the Waldorf."

* * * *

The annual Metropolitan Opera Benefit Ball at the Waldorf Astoria Hotel is a big date on the calendar for New York society. I wiggled into my only halfway formal dress—the plain black sheath—and torturous high heels. One saving grace: the shoes add a few inches to my height. I tried doing something different with my corkscrew hair but abandoned the effort as a lost cause. Thank goodness David and I make a great team at these fancy charity events. He looks sensational in his tux, he knows the names and background stories of every Manhattan celebrity, and he can identify the designers who create all the ladies' gowns. I'm aggressive enough to collar them to answer a few questions.

I grabbed a taxi to the coffee shop on the corner of Park and 49th, across from the Waldorf's front entrance. David and Gene were sipping coffee in a booth by the front door. I scooted in next to Gene. "Are you going with us to the shindig? Between David and me, we could use our press passes to sneak you in."

"Heavens, no. You two go ahead and rub elbows. I'll sit here and read." He held up an accounting textbook.

"When do you take that test? It seems like all you do is study for it."

"End of January. It's important. Maybe I'll pass and get certified to manage rich people's money instead of just taking their pictures. No offense, David."

"None taken." David began gathering his camera equipment. "We'd better get to gettin', darlin'. We don't want to miss any of them early birds."

Yellow taxis and long black limos lined Park Avenue in both directions in front of the hotel's entrance. Half a dozen doormen wearing smart gray uniforms with gold braids across their chests stood at attention, ready to help the ladies in long formal gowns out of their cars.

We waited for the traffic light, and David pulled out his camera. "I want to get a shot of the hotel before all the to-do starts. It's such a wonderful old Art Deco landmark."

That's a thing I love about David. Photography is not just a job to him, it's art.

We pushed through the revolving glass doors and climbed the wide stairs to the ballroom level. A guy wearing a tuxedo and holding a clipboard was checking press passes and herding reporters and print media on the left, and TV and radio on the right. David and I staked out a spot just as the first guests began arriving.

We took up our usual routine. David bent over and whispered, "Laura Stern, heiress to a bourbon fortune, on the board of the Met, married to Gordon Lake. He's gay. She's wearing Dior." He took three or four shots as the couple ascended the steps on a pink carpet installed for the occasion, and I grabbed them at the top of the stairs for a quick interview. The next forty-five minutes went that way with the rest of the city's glitterati arriving for the gala. The murmur from the crowd in the ballroom lobby grew to a buzz then a roar as the place filled and guests started their second cocktails.

The lights flickered, signaling the crowd to find their seats at the round dinner tables in the ballroom and the press to begin packing our equipment. From the corner of my eye, I saw the revolving front door at the bottom of the stairs spin and a couple step through. He was the kind of man who is of average height but looks taller because of the way he carries himself. You may think I'm obsessed with height. Maybe I am. The woman was picture-perfect and beautiful, with impeccably understated makeup, a chic designer gown, and a photogenic smile.

It was like the whole gaggle of press held their breath for a second, then flashbulbs began popping like popcorn. Reporters rushed forward to capture quotes from the couple. I elbowed David. "Who's that?"

"Thomas Putnam, Junior, Tommy to his friends, and his wife, Tina. He's purportedly the youngest billionaire in the United States. The sole owner of the Putnam Real Estate Development Company. She's wearing vintage Chanel."

"They sure know how to make a dramatic entrance."

The ballroom lights flashed again, and Clipboard Guy bustled over to order us out the front door. Thomas Putnam guided his wife up the stairs with a possessive hand on the small of her back like she wouldn't have been able to make it up without his help.

I stepped in front of the couple. "Mrs. Putnam, I'm from the *Gazette.* That's a lovely vintage Chanel you're wearing."

Tommy Putnam took one look at me in my generic black dress and wobbly high heels and guided his wife around me and up the stairs.

Clipboard Guy rushed to the couple. "Mr. and Mrs. Putnam. This way, please. You're seated at the maestro's table. I'll show you the way." And with that, they were whisked away without another glance my way.

"Well, Mr. Tommy Putnam is downright rude."

David nodded. "I guess he's used to being in charge."

Chapter Nine

"BUTCH!"

I jumped and the stack of David's eight-by-ten photos I'd been shuffling through fluttered to the floor. "What?"

Jake leaned across my desk. "Get your head out of the clouds. I'm trying to tell you there's a delivery for you downstairs."

"Thanks." I bent over to retrieve the pictures.

"What're the photos you're so interested in? Some fancy party?"

"The shots David took at the Judge Hawthorne murder scene." I turned one around so he could see it.

Jake peeked at the picture of the body hanging from the ceiling fan. He made a face. "Ugh!"

"Good thing you're a sports reporter. You've got too weak a stomach for the crime beat."

"You're right. I'll leave Harry to it. Anyway, you've got a delivery." He hitched up his pants and sauntered off.

I thumbed through the photos and stopped at the close-up shot of the note tacked to the judge's chest. Walt Smith was at his desk behind me, clacking away on his typewriter. "Walt, do you have a minute?"

"Certainly."

I held the photo up. "Where does this quote come from? 'The sins of the father are to be laid upon the children.'"

"William Shakespeare. *Merchant of Venice*. Act Three, Scene Five. But the thought originally comes from the Bible, as many of Shakespeare's ideas do. It refers to the concept that sin has consequences and that some sins are so evil, they have intergenerational echoes."

"How about this symbol at the bottom? The one that looks like a rifle scope."

Walt took the photo from me and held it close to his face. "It's the Solar Cross. The four tips of the cross represent winter and summer solstice and spring and fall equinox. If the sign were the face of a clock, twelve represents winter solstice, the moment when the earth is tilted farthest away from the sun and the longest night of the year."

He picked up his pen and placed the tip on the circle halfway between ten and eleven on the clock. "We're here right now. Wiccans believe this is the time when the veil between our world and the Otherworld is thinnest. When our departed come back to visit."

"Wiccans are witches, right?"

Walt settled back in his chair, gearing up for a lecture on the ins and outs of witchhood. "In layman's terms, yes."

I picked up the photo. "That's great. Thanks for the info. Very helpful. Guess I've got a delivery downstairs, so I'll get going. Thanks." I scraped back my chair and power walked by Duke Reynold's glass-enclosed office, trying to get past the city editor before he saw me. Didn't make it.

Duke took the cigar stub out of this mouth long enough to growl. "Butch."

He'd be wanting the Met Gala write-up. I hadn't been able to get my mind off Judge Hawthorne long enough to write the article. "On it, boss. Gotta run right now." I pointed toward the exit. "Delivery downstairs."

I walked the four flights down instead of waiting for the elevator. The front desk guard handed me an envelope. No postage and no return address. Just my name on the front in red crayon, ELEANOR TRACY.

The guard held up both hands. "If you're going to ask who delivered it, save your breath. I went to the john, and when I came back the letter was on the desk."

I tore open the envelope. Inside was a Halloween greeting card with cartoon witches circling a boiling cauldron. I opened the card and read the message, printed in comic script, "Something Wicked This Way Comes," and below, handwritten in red crayon, whoever had sent the envelope to me had added, "...AND IT'S ME." There was a letter included, written with the same red crayon.

DEAR MISS TRACY,

YOU MAY WONDER WHY I'M CONTACTING YOU INSTEAD OF HARRY LOGAN SINCE HE WAS THE AUTHOR OF THE FLAWED STORY ABOUT THE JUDGE IN THIS MORNING'S PAPER. HARRY HYPOTHESIZES MY MOTIVE WAS SOME DECISION BY THE JUDGE THAT WENT AGAINST MY INTERESTS. THIS IS NOT THE CASE. YOUR PAPER NEEDS TO LOOK DEEPER. THERE ARE TWO REASONS I'M REACHING OUT TO YOU IN PARTICULAR: FIRST, I FOLLOW YOUR REPORTING. I SAW YOUR BYLINE ON THE DANIA KAPOOR STORY, A VERY TRAGIC AND SENSELESS DEATH. YOUR NAME WAS IN SECOND POSITION, BUT I SUSPECT YOU HAD EVERYTHING TO DO WITH GETTING TO THE BOTTOM OF HER STORY. I THINK YOU ARE THE ONLY JOURNALIST AT YOUR PAPER COMPETENT TO TELL MY TRUE STORY. MY SECOND REASON IS I'VE LOOKED INTO YOUR BACKGROUND. YOU HAVE YOUR OWN PURPOSES FOR SEEKING JUSTICE FOR PAST SINS.

JUDGE HAWTHORNE HAD TO DIE TO PAY FOR THE PAST, THAT MUCH IS TRUE. THERE WILL BE MORE WHO MUST DIE TO SETTLE THE DEBT. I WANT YOU TO BE THE REPORTER WHO WRITES ABOUT WHAT IS TO COME. CALL THE POLICE ABOUT THIS LETTER IF YOU MUST, BUT IF THE NEXT *GAZETTE* STORY DOESN'T HAVE YOUR BYLINE AND YOURS ALONE, I'LL MOVE ON TO THE *TIMES*.

Where the signature would have been, he had drawn the same symbol as on the Hawthorne note, the circle with a cross in it. There was a red dot on the circle between ten and eleven. Was that some kind of clue about the timing of the next murder?

The "past sins" part must have be referred to my upbringing at the orphanage. That was certainly different from most people's experience, but I wouldn't call it being sinned against. In fact, I don't even think about it much anymore since I left Wilmington and came to New York.

Sister Marie Madeline was kind to me. Of course, Sister Margaret Joseph, our mathematics teacher, was a different story. She was the dark side. She whacked my palms with a ruler when I passed notes to the little girl behind me that I had a mad crush on. You know, the kind of notes that say, "I love you, do you love me? Check one: Yes or No." Or if I drifted off into a daydream during the lesson.

I endured the punishment without crying. I didn't want to give Maggie Joe, my secret nickname for the nun, the satisfaction. The spunk that got me nicknamed Butch at the paper was there in my personality from the beginning. I wouldn't call Sister Margaret Joseph a sinner. We fought a battle of wills. I was as much a combatant as she was. Anyway, my mother must have thought leaving me with the nuns was her best choice. I don't think I'm owed a debt, or that I was sinned against. Unless you call bad luck a sin.

How did this guy know about my life in Wilmington anyway?

The front desk guard cleared his throat. "Could you move it to the side? I've got customers lining up behind you."

"Oh, sorry." I stepped away from the reception desk and turned the Halloween card over in my hand. What now? Do I take the card and letter to the police or to Harry or to my boss? Harry first. I ran up the stairs two at a time, waved through the glass at the boss without making eye contact, and found Harry smoking a cigarette with his feet on his desk.

"Harry, I have to talk to you. Look at this."

He raised his eyebrows at the card, then read the letter. He laid them carefully on his desk. "Well, first of all, we shouldn't be touching these. The cops will go over them for fingerprints, though I doubt they'll find any. I wouldn't be surprised if this guy knows something about police procedure. He probably wore gloves."

"You think we should take the letter to the police?"

"Eventually. The question is when. Do we run the story about the letter first? We need to talk to Duke." He pushed back his chair and led the way to Duke's office. I checked my watch. The editor would just have finished putting the evening edition to bed.

Duke was reading the *New York Times*. His face changed when he saw both Harry and me walk into his office. He laid the paper aside and squared his shoulders. A city editor solves problems all day, what reporters to assign where, what story leads on the front page above the fold, and how to keep the paper out of libel trouble. Duke must have guessed we were bringing him some problem to solve.

"Yeah?"

Harry gestured toward the *Times*. "Reading the competition, boss? Take a look at this." He passed the card and letter across the desk.

Duke read them twice, took the cigar stub out of his mouth, and tossed it across the room into a wastebasket. "He's threatening to go to the *Times*, huh?"

The Judge Hawthorne story was right up our alley at the *Gazette*. For sure, Duke wouldn't want to lose out to the *Times* on such a juicy story. He leaned back in his chair. "Who at NYPD caught the Hawthorne case?"

"Mike Sloane from the Ninth."

I waited a beat. "And Detective Carr."

Duke looked at me as though he had forgotten for a minute I was in the room. "Have you told anyone about this letter?"

"No. It was delivered downstairs. The guard didn't see who."

"We'll run the story in the evening edition tomorrow on page one. Call Sloane at noon tomorrow, and I'll call the Police Commissioner at twelve fifteen. They'll know the story's coming, but too late to stop it. Now get busy and write it." He tossed the card and letter across the desk and went back to reading the *Times*.

Harry and I looked at each other. "Whose story is it?"

Duke didn't look up. "Butch's."

We started out the door. "And Butch, I'm still waiting for the Met Gala piece."

I followed Harry back to his desk. "I hope you know I'm not trying to cut you out of the story."

Harry waved me away. "Don't worry. This guy, whoever he is, decided for all of us. You take the byline and run with it, otherwise we give the scoop to the competition. If you need any help, let me know. Till then, I'll stay out of it. I'll call Sloane tomorrow and tell him we're printing the story with the letter, and you're on the piece."

"He'll be upset we're making the letter public, especially since he went out on a limb to let us into the crime scene."

"He'll get over it. We're doing our job like he's doing his."

"What do you think about the letter writer saying we got the motive wrong?"

"Sloane seems pretty sure about it. He's like a bloodhound when he gets on the scent. Anyone has his work cut out for him trying to change his mind."

When I got back to my desk, the phone was ringing. It was David.

"Hey, darlin'. Want to share a cab home tonight?"

"Can't. Duke handed me the Judge Hawthorne story, and I still have the Met Gala to finish. This will be a late night."

"Wait, did you say you got the Hawthorne story? By yourself? How did that happen?"

"It's too long to tell you right now, but if you're still up when I get home, I'll fill you in."

"This is the break you've been waiting for after the Kapoor story. Why don't you sound more excited?"

"I am. I just have a nagging feeling there's more to the judge's murder than Detective Sloane thinks. He's working on the theory that the judge was killed as revenge by someone he sent to prison. I'll need to get an angle on the motive to write the complete story."

"Knock on the door when you get home. We'll still be up. Tonight's *Columbo*, and you know Gene never misses the show."

Chapter Ten

THE 9TH PRECINCT POLICE station is a six-story building in the middle of the block on Centre Street. The desk sergeant at the entrance looked up from the usual paperwork to check my press pass. He peered over the edge of the elevated desk and looked me up and down. "And who's expecting you?"

"I'm here to see Detective Sloane." I held up a manila envelope. After I had copied the letter and Halloween card, I decided to hand deliver the originals to the precinct instead of trusting them to a bicycle messenger. Bringing them in person might also give me a chance to mend a fence with Sloane if he was upset about the paper printing the details from the letter.

The sergeant picked up the phone and dialed. "Sloane in?" He hung up the receiver and shook his head. "He's out."

Great. An excuse to talk to Detective Carr. "What about Detective Carr?"

The sergeant blew a frustrated breath and went through the phone routine again. He pointed up the stairs. "Detective squad room is on the fifth floor."

The detectives' bullpen smelled like cigarette smoke and Aqua Velva. A receptionist's desk blocked the entrance. She was pecking away on an ancient typewriter that appeared to have a sticking problem because she stopped every few strokes and swore under her breath. Her hair was a shade of red that does not occur in nature.

I bent down to catch her eye. "I'm here to see Detective Carr."

She pointed to a desk in the corner across the room.

I recognized the back of Detective Carr's head. She had her desk positioned so she could see out the windows overlooking Centre Street. "Should I just go over, or what?"

The receptionist waved her hand without looking up. "Help yourself."

I wound my way between mismatched desks with detectives on the phone or typing on official-looking forms. They weren't uniformed cops, but they had their own version of uniforms: white dress shirts with rolled-up sleeves and slack neckties, gray fedoras, and cigarettes hanging out of their mouths. Detective Carr stuck out like a sore thumb. She was the only woman, number one, and her crisp white blouse looked fresh, like she'd just picked it up from the laundry.

Stacks of paper covered her desk. As I got closer, I could see they were logs. She held a logbook in her lap studying the handwritten entries. I figured Sloane had her trying to match the judge's cases with guys recently released from prison. I was sure she was wasting her time. The killer put that notion in doubt when he said Harry's story in the *Gazette* was wrong. Looked like busywork to me.

I cleared my throat. "Detective Carr."

She turned around. The same wisp of dark hair I noticed at the Dania Kapoor scene had escaped her tight bun. I wondered if she ever wore her hair loose.

She slammed the book in her lap shut.

"I didn't mean to interrupt. The receptionist appeared to have her hands full. She said to come on over."

Carr motioned toward a straight chair next to her desk. "Yes, Dot is not the friendliest person you'll ever meet. The guys joke she was voted Miss Congeniality in the 1946 Miss Staten Island beauty pageant."

"I guess you saw the paper last night." I pulled the letter and card from the manila envelope and laid them on her desk. "This is the letter from the killer. The print in red crayon appears to match the note pinned to the judge's body. The note left at the scene talks about 'sins of the father' and the letter refers to payment 'for the past.' Doesn't that imply the motive must be retribution for some act of Hawthorne's father, not anything about the judge himself?"

She picked up the letter. "Sloane isn't convinced. He still thinks the killer is someone the judge sentenced to prison. This print does appear to match the note. I can run the letter by the lab for their expert opinion as soon as I finish these logs."

"That could take you a week, and there might be another murder in the meantime. The killer says as much." I grabbed the letter out of her hand, maybe a little too forcefully. "See, he says right here, 'There will be more who must die...'"

"Good police work is all about the details, and it takes time and careful focus."

"So you said on the bridge the other day, but don't you ever just get a feeling in your gut and go with it?"

"It doesn't work like that. You've seen way too many TV detective shows."

I got a picture of Gene watching *Columbo*. "Maybe we could team up. I could help you go through the logs and get that out of the way."

She looked around the bullpen. "I can't have a reporter sitting in the station working on my case. Besides, I'm not sure I can trust you. What's to keep whatever you see from winding up on the front page of the *Gazette* like this letter did?"

"If you want to talk trust, I don't trust Sloane to solve this case before the killer strikes again. And who knows? Public awareness may help develop leads. It's happened before. If you don't want me helping you here in the station, bring the logs to my apartment tonight. It's not as though they're evidence. It's research at this point. I'll order in Chinese, and we can power through them in a few hours."

I figured the sooner Detective Carr got through the logs, the more likely Sloane would consider another motive. Also, getting to know her would be nice. And having her to my apartment was much better than just getting a phone number. Two birds with one stone.

Carr's finger tapped the log on her lap while she considered my offer. "I agree the motive in this case might not be as simple as Sloane thinks. There's something about that note." I watched her mentally run the risk/reward analysis of letting me help with the logs. She tucked the strand of hair behind her ear. "What's your address?"

I scratched my nose to hide a grin as I rattled off my address. "How about tonight at seven?"

* * * *

I hurried home from work to clean the bathroom and generally spruce up my apartment in anticipation of Detective Carr coming over. I stood in the middle of the floor and turned in a circle, imagining seeing the place through her eyes. She was sure to be impressed. It's beautiful.

Not that I'm great at decorating. The furnishings are sparse. An old leather couch I picked up at the flea market that I like to think has character. Next to the couch an old, you could call it vintage, magazine rack with my police band radio. There's a hand-me-down blond wood coffee table Gene and David passed along and a bed with no headboard in the corner. In the kitchen area, a huge butcher block island that used to belong to a real butcher has two stools and serves triple duty as counter space, dining table, and work area. Detective Carr might not be impressed with my taste, but she had to appreciate the work David and Gene had done to renovate the old brownstone.

Detective Carr's knock interrupted my obsessing about making a good impression on her. I checked the clock. Exactly seven. *She's prompt.* I took a last look around and opened the door. The detective and David stood on the landing. She wore her "civies," jeans and a sky-blue sweater that matched her eyes. Her hair fell in waves to her shoulders. That answered my question about whether she ever wore it loose. She flashed that dazzling smile I'd seen at the Coast Guard pier.

David juggled a stack of three cardboard boxes full of logs. "Look who I found downstairs."

"Come in, Detective Carr."

She took one of the boxes off the stack and stepped into the room. "Please call me Christine." This was going to work out great.

I took another box off David's stack. "I see you met David. You may remember him as the photographer from the *Gazette*."

"Yes, I remember." She set her box down. "Thanks, David."

"My pleasure, Christine." He set the last box down inside the door. Behind her back, he winked and gave me a thumbs-up. I shooed him away and closed the door.

Christine looked around. "Wonderful place. I'm still living at the Barbizon. I haven't had time since I moved from Buffalo to even start looking for an apartment."

"The Barbizon. That's the hotel for women where they don't allow men above the ground floor, right?"

"Yes. Not a problem for me."

Did she give me a significant sideways look or was it my wishful thinking? I led the way to the butcher block counter. "I thought we'd set up over here and get started. I can order Chinese when we're hungry."

We settled into a system, checking recent releases from New York state prisons against the handwritten lists of Judge Hawthorne's daily court calendars for the last ten years. It was tedious going and frustrating since I was convinced we were barking up the wrong tree. By midnight, we had finished two of the three boxes without any matches. We had gotten nearly to the bottom of the last box when Christine found something.

She circled a name. "I got one. Released from Bedford Hills two weeks before the murder. Edwina K. Stone. Sentenced to fifteen years for dealing heroin, released on probation after seven."

"A woman! Funny, from the letter he sent me, I assumed a man. Something about his tone. Could it be possible? Could a woman pull off the Hawthorne hanging?"

"Rare, but it wouldn't be the first time. Hanging would fit what we usually see with female killers. They tend to prefer bloodless methods instead of stabbing or shooting."

"What happens now that you have a name?"

"The probation officer will know her whereabouts. Sloane and I will bring her in for questioning." She started packing the logs back into the boxes.

"Hey wait a minute. I'll open a bottle of wine. We can relax for a while."

She checked her watch. "Have to pass. I'll get in the office early. Sloane's attention will be on getting Edwina K. Stone into the station for questioning. I can go ahead and check on the printing in the murder note against your letter."

I helped her repack the last of the logs. "I'll see what I can find in the *Gazette* clippings morgue about Judge Hawthorne's father. Maybe there's some clue about his sins like the note says."

We hauled the boxes down the stairs, and I waited while she hailed a cab.

David must have been watching out the window. His door flew open as I started up the stairs. "She's cute." He drew out the last syllable in his Mississippi accent. "And she's into you, baybee."

I shrugged. "You think so? I don't know."

"I'm never wrong about these things."

"I'll keep that thought. I've got a perfectly good bottle of wine that needs drinking. Want a glass?"

Between us, David and I finished the bottle, and I fell into bed fully clothed at two in the morning.

Chapter Eleven

THE FIRST THING THE next morning, I rode a service elevator down to the clippings morgue in the subbasement of the *Gazette* building, two levels below the city. There's no natural light down there and no sound from the street above, just the constant flickering and buzzing of fluorescent tubes and the steady drip of leaky pipes. From the humble surroundings, you might think the paper doesn't value a hundred years of history in the archives, but that's not true. The morgue is down in the subbasement because it has to be on bedrock to support the weight of 4000 metal file cabinet drawers housing five or six million newspaper clips. Scotty, the guy who runs the morgue, told me he estimates the weight at 600,000 to 700,000 pounds of paper. Don't know how he came up with that, but I'll take his word. He knows more about the morgue than anyone alive.

I've gotten well acquainted with the place while researching articles about wealthy socialites. Scotty said once, "The great thing about the clippings morgue is you can find what you did not know you were looking for."

The nerve center of the morgue, I guess you could think of it as the brain, is the card catalog like the one in a library. Hundreds of little drawers full of typewritten index cards cataloging the clips files according to person and incident. Look up anything or anybody you can think of, and if it's made the newspaper the card catalog will lead you to the original article stored in the vast maze of file cabinets lining the aisles.

Scotty glanced up from his desk when I opened the heavy metal front door. He was cutting articles from the morning edition of the *Gazette*, wearing his usual starched white shirt, bow tie, and a dark suit with a bright red pocket square. He is the sharpest dresser at the paper, stuck away in the basement where no one from the public ever sees him. He beckoned with his scissors. "Butch, come in. What can I do for you today?"

"I'm looking for background on the murder of Judge John Hawthorne. I caught the assignment from Duke."

"Good for you. A promotion of sorts."

"Yes."

"How can I help?"

"I need anything we have on the judge's father."

"You're trying to track down the sins of the father referenced in the killer's note."

"That's right. Do you read all the articles you clip out and file away, Scotty? And is it true that every name mentioned in the paper is clipped and cataloged? How is that possible?"

"This newspaper is my passion." He gestured at the crew of six clerks, busy clipping and cataloging articles. "As long as we keep up with each edition that comes out, we're good."

"The paper's lucky to have you."

"The boys upstairs keep talking about replacing all the file cabinets with an IBM computer. As soon as the technology gets a bit cheaper, you'll walk in the door and shake hands with a machine. That's when I retire." He looked around the cavernous space. "I don't know. There's something magical about holding the actual newspaper article in your hand. I suppose someday we won't have real newspapers or even real books." He smiled. "But you didn't come all the way underground to hear me philosophize. How can I help you with the judge's case?"

"The police are convinced the killer had some personal grievance against the judge, but I'm thinking if that's true, why the quote thumbtacked to his chest that suggests it was something his father did?"

"Interesting question." Scotty folded the newspaper he was working on and held up his hands. His fingers were black with ink from newsprint. "Messy fingers are a hazard of the profession. Let me wash up, and I'll be right with you."

He came back and grabbed a pad and pencil. "Now, the father's name?"

"I don't exactly have the name yet. I thought maybe I could look in the Advance Obit drawer. It might have the deceased's obit listing the parents." The paper keeps two file cabinets with pre-written obits of living prominent people, in case he or she dies unexpectedly. Kind of creepy.

"As a matter of fact, the obit writer came down last evening. I believe he did find the judge. Follow me." He led me to the black metal four-drawer file cabinets with handmade signs taped to the front, labeling them *Advance Obits*. "They're filed by alpha, as you can see." He opened the H drawer and thumbed through folders. "Ah! Here it is. Your murder victim. Judge John Cranfield Hawthorne." He scanned the typed page. A delighted smile lit up his face. "Eureka!" You have to admire a guy who loves his job as much as Scotty.

"Judge Hawthorne was preceded in death by his parents, Dr. Jackson Bradford Hawthorne, Professor Emeritus and noted Chaucer scholar at Columbia University, and Alice Cranfield Hawthorne. He was the great-grandson of nineteenth-century novelist Nathaniel Hawthorne."

He led the way to the card files. "Let's see if we can find clips for the father, Professor Emeritus Hawthorne." He wheeled a ladder over, climbed near the top, pulled an index card, and climbed down. "Here we are." I trailed after him as he searched a long row of file cabinets until he found the one with Professor Hawthorne's folder of clips. My breathing sped up as he opened it. A lone article fluttered to the floor, and I picked it up. "It's from 1942." I read the headline aloud. "'Benefactor Endows Chair at Columbia.' An anonymous donor gave Columbia two million dollars to establish the Jackson Bradford Hawthorne Chair in Early English Literature."

Scotty raised his eyebrows. "If you're looking for sins, this is hardly the dossier of a sinful man. You could try the Columbia English Department. You might turn up something. Could be his sins were not the kind that show up in the newspaper."

"Good idea, Scotty. Thanks."

I hustled over to the Columbia campus. The English department is in Philosophy Hall, one of the oldest buildings at the university. In the small plaza in front of the building, the last stubborn red and gold leaves were losing their battle to hang on to the branches of skeletal maple trees. A larger than life-sized copy of Rodin's *The Thinker* guarded the front door. I figured the sculpture was meant to inspire students to contemplate deep philosophical thoughts. The directory inside the front door listed the Chairman of the English Department's office on the sixth floor.

I took the stairs and found the office. Gold letters etched into the glass door announced "Chairman of the Columbia Department of English and Comparative Literature. James T. O'Leary, PhD." The James T. O'Leary part was twice as big as the rest. This guy must have a healthy ego.

Inside, the office was deserted except for a middle-aged woman at a typewriter. She looked up and smiled pleasantly. "Good morning. May I help you?"

I handed her a card. "I'm a reporter with the *Gazette*. I don't have an appointment, but I'm hoping to speak with Dr. O'Leary."

She hesitated a moment. "Have a seat, dear. I'll check."

She went to the door of an inside office, knocked lightly, and opened it a few inches. A deep male voice boomed out, "Mrs. Nash. I thought I made it abundantly clear I'm not to be disturbed. You know I'm preparing for my luncheon speech at the Union Club today. Do you see the time? It's after eleven already. If your job has become too much for you, I suggest you consider taking advantage of the university's generous retirement program."

She backed up a step. "I know, Dr. O'Leary, but it's a reporter from the *Gazette*. You always want to talk to reporters."

"Why didn't you say so? Show him in."

Mrs. Nash turned back to me, her face burning scarlet from embarrassment. I mouthed, *Sorry*. She nodded and motioned I should go into the office.

Dr. James T. O'Leary stood behind his desk with a big smile that faded when he saw I wasn't the tall male reporter he expected. His expression almost made me laugh. I stuck out my hand. "Eleanor Tracy from the *Gazette*."

He recovered his composure, offered me a seat on a brown leather sofa, one in a lot better shape than the flea market version in my apartment, and settled beside me. Floor-to-ceiling walnut shelves filled with important-looking books lined his office. The whole thing looked staged, like the books were not actually there to be read, and if you tried to pull one out you'd open a trap door hiding a safe, like in the movies.

O'Leary crossed his legs and straightened the crease in his trousers. "We are always happy to meet with the press." He was the kind of guy who said we when he meant I.

"It's important the public know about our distinguished faculty and their truly groundbreaking research. The university touts breakthroughs in science, medicine, and economics, but discoveries in the arts are just as important." He looked around the room and took a mock conspiratorial tone. "In fact, I can give you an important story. I think you newspaper people call it a scoop. Today, I'm delivering an address at the Union Club, very exclusive. Our president is proposing me for membership." He glanced at me sideways. "The president of Columbia University."

I knew he wasn't talking about the president of the United States.

"I'm addressing the membership of the Union Club about a heretofore unknown Shakespearean manuscript, discovered in the main library at Oxford by one of our faculty, Dr. Cathcart. He holds the Hawthorne Chair in Early English Literature."

"I came to ask you about Professor Hawthorne."

"Absolutely beloved. What a gentleman, and the world's greatest expert on Chaucer."

"You heard about his son's murder."

"Yes, tragic."

"You knew Professor Hawthorne personally?"

"Very well. He was my dissertation adviser. He passed away the next year, my first as a junior faculty member. Found dead of a heart attack in the stacks at Butler Library." He sighed and gazed out the window across the tops of the maple trees. "Dr. Hawthorne's death was a great loss to the department."

"So, you were around when the two-million-dollar donation came in to create the Hawthorne Chair. Quite the cause for celebration around the department, I suspect. Do you know the identity of the donor?"

He shot me a smarmy smile meant to say, *I'd love to tell you, but my hands are tied.*

"The donor wished to remain anonymous, and it's strict university policy to honor his request."

"You called Professor Hawthorne beloved. Do you know of anyone who would have a reason to disagree, who might hold a grudge against him? Maybe a former student?"

He straightened his trouser leg again, his tell when he was being careful with his words. "As I said, he was universally beloved. Now, if there's nothing more, I really must get back to preparing for my presentation. I wish I could invite you to hear it firsthand, however..." The smarmy smile again.

I stood up. "Women are not allowed at the Union Club."

"Yes. Unfortunately."

"Thanks for your time."

He led me to the door. "My pleasure. Anytime. As I said, we always love to meet with members of the media."

Mrs. Nash followed me into the hallway and pressed a small, folded piece of paper into my palm then scurried back into the office.

The handwritten note said, "Julia Rains. She's a teacher at PS Fifty-Five."

I made a quick trip by the newsroom to answer some Dear Aunt Betty letters and let Duke know I was still alive. I found Walt leaning back in his chair, working on his daily crossword puzzle. "Greetings, Eleanor. Any news from your lady police friend about the judge's killer?"

"They're on the trail of a woman recently paroled from Bedford Hills. Judge Hawthorne sent her to prison, and Detective Carr's partner thinks the perp might have taken her revenge when she got released."

"Perp! You are beginning to sound like a real crime reporter. You appear skeptical about this perp being the guilty party."

"I don't know. I don't see the connection with 'sins of the father.'"

"What does Detective Carr think?"

"Carr is working under Sloane right now. She's new to NYPD. She might have her ideas about the case, but she's deferring to him. He's got her looking for people who might hold a grudge against the judge about a decision he made."

"Sounds reasonable. Well, good luck to you both." He went back to his crossword puzzle.

I finished the Aunt Betty column, dropped it in my outbox, and grabbed a cab to Public School 55 in the Bronx, just north of Yankee Stadium. A light rain shrouded the liver-colored brick walls of the four-story building. The surrounding tall black wrought iron fence created the atmosphere of a prison. As I crossed the asphalt playground, marked off for four square and basketball, a loud bell rang, and a tide of kids spilled out the front door. Behind them, older students sauntered down the steps, much too cool to show their exuberance at being set free.

One of the kids directed me to Miss Rains's third-floor classroom. The teacher was erasing the blackboard with her back to the open door. "Miss Rains?"

She turned toward my voice. She was tall. Her dark, naturally curly hair was cut short and sprinkled with gray. Her slim tan skirt and patterned blouse flattered her trim figure. She was a handsome woman, her features too strong to be called pretty.

I pointed to the blackboard. "I see your students are diagramming sentences. I used to love diagramming. So orderly. Every word and phrase in its place and accounted for like a jigsaw puzzle."

"Yes, some students enjoy it. Others find the exercises too fidgety." She laid the eraser aside and dusted her hands together. "Can I help you?"

I offered my hand. "I'm a reporter from the *Gazette*. Butch Tracy. I got your name from Mrs. Nash in the English department at Columbia."

She declined the handshake, showing me her palms still dusty with chalk. "Mrs. Nash is a lovely woman."

"She was very kind and helpful. I'm following up on an aspect of Judge John Hawthorne's murder."

"I read about it, but I didn't know him. I'm not clear how you think I can help."

"The killer left a clue at the scene, a note that said, 'The sins of the father are to be laid upon the children.'"

"He's a Shakespeare fan?"

"The murderer might mean he killed Judge Hawthorne as payback for the sins of his father, Professor Jackson Bradford Hawthorne. Did you know him?"

The radiator under the large double-hung windows banged with three metallic clangs. Julia Rains walked to the window and raised it a few inches, letting a draft blow across the classroom. "I like to air things out this time of the year. The smell of wet wool and chalk dust can become overwhelming." She took a sweater from the back of her desk chair, draped it over her shoulders, and leaned against the front edge of her desk. "Dr. Hawthorne was my dissertation adviser at Columbia."

I sat at a student desk in the front row. "As he was for Dr. O'Leary, the current department chairman. Was that at the same time?"

"Yes."

"So, I should more accurately call you Dr. Rains?"

"No, I didn't complete my doctorate. What did O'Leary tell you about Professor Hawthorne?"

"He called him a beloved and valued member of the English department. He said Dr. Hawthorne was his dissertation adviser. I asked about who donated the two million dollars for the Hawthorne Chair. He said it's Columbia's policy to maintain the donor's anonymity. Can you tell me about your connection with Professor Hawthorne? Do you know about the donation?"

She folded her arms and hugged them to her body and stared at the back of the classroom. "In 1942, America had just gotten into the war, and several of the Columbia departments lifted their ban on women to keep their graduate student ranks full. I studied Chaucerian literature with Dr. Hawthorne and wrote my dissertation on Chaucer's use of Middle English in his works when everyone else was still writing in French and Latin. Almost two thousand English words are first attested to Chaucerian manuscripts." She seemed to suddenly remember I was in the room. She chuckled. "Sorry to bore you with my rambling about arcane things."

"I appreciate your taking the time to talk with me."

She nodded. "Dr. Hawthorne worked closely with me all along the process of my research for my dissertation. He was so helpful every step of the way. He seemed truly proud to be my sponsor. He never made me feel less than for being female."

I began to get the sinking feeling Julia Rains would be a dead end in my quest to discover the father's sins that might have gotten Judge Hawthorne killed. I wondered why Mrs. Nash in the chairman's office steered me her way.

She pushed up from her desk and paced. "Two days before I was to present my paper to the dissertation committee, someone stole my work from my apartment, along with all my notes and research. I was hysterical. I lived with three other women at the time. There was no way to know who might have gotten access to my papers. I immediately tried contacting Dr. Hawthorne. He didn't answer his phone, and his office was locked and dark. Mrs. Nash tried helping me appeal to anyone in power who could put off the committee meeting until I could do something, anything, I didn't know what. Hawthorne was the only other person in the world who knew about my research. It was no use in the end. The committee met as I lay in my apartment practically in a coma of misery."

"Did you report the theft to the police?"

"Yes. I got the distinct impression the disappearance of a bunch of papers would go to the bottom of their priority list behind murders and burglaries. Besides, the mystery of what happened to my work got solved quickly. James O'Leary submitted my dissertation to the committee as his own, and he became James O'Leary, PhD. His father, Shamus O'Leary, a multi-millionaire rum-runner, donated two million dollars in Professor Hawthorne's name to Columbia, a powerful inducement for Hawthorne's silence."

"You mean a bribe."

"Yes. For a man like Professor Hawthorne at the end of his career, the prospect of immortality was too tempting to pass up. The president of Columbia launched a halfhearted investigation based on my accusations. Even that was dropped when Professor Hawthorne retired as emeritus and died a few months later."

"Horrible." Something Walt Smith said came back to my mind. *Sin has consequences, and some sins are so evil they leave intergenerational echoes.* "Professor Hawthorne, who you thought was your mentor, did an evil thing. You must have felt personally assaulted."

"I did for a while, but I moved on. I had to support myself, so I applied for a position in the public school system and became an eighth-grade English teacher." She looked around the room. "That seems like yesterday, but I've been here almost thirty years. In a way, it all turned out for the best. I don't think I would have been satisfied with the life of an academic, stuck in some dim library, breathing the dust from centuries-old manuscripts. Even if Columbia had offered me a faculty position, a big 'if' in those days."

"James O'Leary seems to be thriving."

"O'Leary is a politician, not an academic."

A soft knock interrupted her. A youngish woman with a blond ponytail stood in the doorway. She wore sweatpants with a whistle around her neck. She looked from Miss Rains to me and back to her. "I'm sorry to interrupt. Are you going to be a while, Julie? Should I wait, or go on home?"

I stood up from the student desk. "I've taken enough of your time."

Miss Rains began straightening papers on her desk. "This is Miss Tracy, a reporter from the *Gazette*. I think we're about done. Wait for me."

The blonde nodded. "I'll be in the teachers' lounge." She gave me a last glance and disappeared around the corner.

Miss Rains closed the window. She used more force than necessary, and a bang echoed across the empty classroom. She stood with her hands on her hips, gazing over the wet asphalt below. "Looks like it's raining in earnest now. Your best bet for a taxi is on Webster."

Either my questions had raised painful memories for her, or she was holding more anger in the present than she let on, or both. Could she have murdered Hawthorne? Maybe. She was fit enough, and her athletic friend could have helped. I hoped she wasn't the killer. I liked her, and she certainly had been wronged back in 1942. If she was responsible for Judge Hawthorne's death, why seek revenge on his father by murdering the son thirty years later?

Instead of hailing a cab, I ducked into a phone booth on the corner. The stuffy space smelled like the school kids' wet wool clothes, just as Julia said. I dialed the 9th Precinct. Miss Congeniality connected me with Christine.

"Carr."

"Christine, it's Butch. I've found someone who might have a serious grudge against Judge Hawthorne's father like the note on his body said. Her name is Julia Rains. She's a teacher here at PS Fifty-Five."

"Hold on, hold on, Butch. Did you say you're at the school now? Did you talk to her?"

"Yes. That note pinned to the judge has to mean something, doesn't it? I'm trying to figure out what. Don't you think you should at least hear her story?" Silence on the other end. I may have stepped over a line. "I mean, maybe you could meet with her and see what you think."

"Sloane is convinced we have our killer, Edwina K. Stone. We're running that down now." I pictured Christine tucking that wisp of hair behind her ear while she considered her next sentence. "I suppose questioning Julia Rains couldn't hurt."

* * * *

Christine arranged to meet Julia Rains at a coffee shop near Yankee Stadium early the next morning. After some convincing, the detective agreed I could be there too. My rationale was I had found Julia Rains in the first place, I would be as quiet as a church mouse, and I would consider anything Rains said "deep background." I wasn't entirely sure what that meant, but I'd heard Harry use it to reassure reluctant witnesses. I thought it meant I wouldn't quote Julia in any newspaper articles.

Julia arrived on time. She slid into the booth across from us, folded her hands on the Formica tabletop, and waited.

"I'm Detective Carr, NYPD, and you already know Miss Tracy. I appreciate your meeting us on such short notice."

Julia nodded. "I'm not sure how I can help. As I told Miss Tracy, I didn't know Judge Hawthorne."

"But you knew his father, Professor Jackson Hawthorne?"

"Yes."

Christine placed a folder on the table in front of Julia and opened it. "This is a copy of a police report dated June 2, 1942. Is that your signature at the bottom?"

"Yes."

"The report says someone stole your dissertation. Can you tell me what happened?"

Julia repeated the story she told me in her classroom the day before, including the part about it being a good thing for her in the long run.

"Where were you, Miss Rains, on Tuesday a week ago around seven in the evening?"

Julia thought a second. "I was participating in Parents' Night at the school."

"What times did that cover?"

"I stayed after classes were done at three thirty, preparing for the parents to start arriving at about five o'clock. When I finally turned off the lights and closed my classroom door, it was ten minutes after nine."

"How do you remember the time so precisely?"

"Have you ever attended a Parents' Night, Detective Carr? The time doesn't exactly fly by. I checked the clock over my blackboard often during the evening, and I was relieved and exhausted when the last parent left. I went right home and fell into bed."

"Can someone vouch for that?"

"My roommate, Meg Ward."

Chapter Twelve

THE JANGLING PHONE SAT me straight up in bed. My alarm clock's luminous dial said 6:12. It was Detective Carr. "Butch, there's been another murder." Are all murders discovered at the crack of dawn? I had gone to bed worried Christine might be upset with me for sending her on a wild goose chase after Julia Rains. Good sign. She was still including me.

She sounded breathless. "I'm headed there now. He's somebody important I think."

I coughed and for some unknown reason tried to sound like I hadn't been asleep. "Where? What's the address?"

She gave me a street number on Fifth Avenue in midtown.

"Is the murderer our guy...or gal?"

"Looks like."

"On my way."

"And Butch, don't mention I called you."

I took a quick shower as cold as I could stand, threw on some clothes, and ran down the stairs to David and Gene's door.

David and I headed downtown to 666 Fifth Avenue, a fifteen-story office building under construction. Five squad cruisers with lights flashing diverted cars and foot traffic off Fifth Avenue. David and I jumped out of the cab and ran the last two blocks to the police cordon. A burly uniformed cop blocked us. "Hold on, girlie."

I flashed my press pass.

"Don't matter. Orders are to keep everyone back."

I caught sight of Detective Carr waiting to board a construction elevator. "Detective Carr!"

She motioned to the uniform and yelled across the sidewalk. "Let them through."

The cop shrugged and stepped aside.

I greeted Carr with a nod. She looked great, as always, even at the early hour. One of the top buttons of her usual cotton blouse was open. It was just enough to show a peek of cleavage. Aren't breasts wonderful? The elevator door swung open, and a uniformed cop motioned us inside. The four of us and David's gear crowded onto the spindly elevator car meant for two people at most. Sometimes my small size is a plus. The car rose up the side of the building, rattling and swaying. I've never trusted the safety of those things. We lurched to a stop on the top floor. In the middle of the bare concrete space, a circle of floodlights erected by forensics technicians lit a neatly stacked pile of cinder blocks. A bright yellow hard hat stuck out from the bottom of the pile. It was attached to a man's head.

Detective Sloane was on the scene already, questioning a beefy, grizzled construction worker and making notes in his little spiral notebook. David unpacked his camera equipment and started popping flashbulbs, and I found a spot where I could overhear Sloane without inviting too much notice.

The worker took his right hand out of his pocket. There was a hook where his hand should be. Would Sloane think that let him off as a suspect? Could a man with only one hand lift all those cinder blocks? "Joe Mirelli. M-I-R-E-L-L-I. I'm the foreman. I'm the one called it in."

Sloane wrote the name in his book. "What time did you find him, Mr. Mirelli?"

"I stepped off the elevator at five thirty sharp as usual. The blocks were here, just like you see them. At first, I thought some of the guys had stacked them up, but then I saw the head. I didn't touch anything. I called 9-1-1 right away."

"Wait here, Mr. Mirelli."

Sloane and Carr and several uniform cops began unstacking the blocks. They were sweating by the time they got down to a panel of plywood covering the body. Sloane tipped it up. I moved closer to peek over his shoulder. Underneath the thin sheet of wood was a dead man in his middle thirties, dressed in blue jeans, work boots, and a flannel shirt with the sleeves rolled up. You would think with all that weight stacked on top of it the body would be flat as a pancake, but he looked pretty normal except that his face had a startled expression with staring eyes and an open mouth. It was covered with a thick layer of gray cement dust. I leaned in to get a closer look. "That's Tommy Putnam. I just saw him a few nights ago at the Met Gala. Him and his wife, Tina." He looked far different from the in-charge guy who guided his wife up the Waldorf staircase at the fancy event.

Sloane turned around. "Tommy Putnam, the billionaire?"

I pressed in closer. "Yep. The youngest billionaire in the United States." I looked at David for confirmation, and he nodded.

A note rested on the corpse's chest, written in big block letters and the same hand as the note tacked to the judge's body. The paper said PREPARE SLAUGHTER FOR HIS CHILDREN FOR THE INIQUITY OF THEIR FATHERS; THAT THEY DO NOT RISE, NOR POSSESS THE LAND, NOR FILL THE FACE OF THE WORLD WITH CITIES.

The killer was right about Putnam rising and possessing the world, at least the part of the world Manhattan accounts for. I did some research on him for my Met Gala piece. He was the city's biggest real estate developer. In just the few years since the son took over The Putnam Company from his father, he had built a reputation for ruthless dealmaking and the ability to turn a profit through all the real estate market's ups and downs. It was also rumored he was slow to pay his debts to subcontractors and suppliers. That could have got him killed, but what about the "iniquity of their fathers" part of the note?

Sloane called Mirelli over. "Do you recognize him?"

"That's..." Mirelli's voice broke, and he swallowed. "It's the owner, Mr. Putnam."

"Have you worked for him a while?"

"I started with his father, Mr. Putnam, Senior, and I've worked for Tommy since he took over the company."

"What was Mr. Putnam doing on the building site dressed like a workman?"

"He comes after the last shift every night to check our progress."

"So, he was here routinely. He sounds like a very hands-on boss."

Mirelli nodded. "He must have been here under those cement blocks since last night."

Construction workers with their lunch buckets and hard hats under their arms started arriving and crowding around the body. Sloane spoke to Carr. "Shoo them out and post a uniform at the bottom by the elevator. No work today."

The elevator rattled to a stop behind us, and Dr. Harkness got off. She opened her bag and took out latex gloves and a notebook. "What have you got for us today, Sloane? Never a dull moment." She circled the body and pointed to the stack of cinder blocks. "Those fell on him?"

"They were neatly stacked on top of him before we moved them."

"That's a new one."

She walked around the blocks, counting them. She hefted one. "That's about right. I count twenty-five blocks, each weighing thirty pounds or so. The human body can withstand seven hundred pounds if it's added gradually. Whoever did this took his time." She lifted the corpse's arm. "I don't see any sign of restraints or defensive wounds. The killer must have subdued the victim somehow. I don't have the tox screen back from Hawthorne yet, but I'll bet we find some kind of anesthetic agent in both of them."

"So, you think the murders are related?"

"That's your territory, Sloane, not mine. But it's a heck of a coincidence if they aren't, wouldn't you say? The judge's postmortem didn't show any signs of struggle either."

"Putnam's time of death?"

"Well, that's going to be a tough call. I'd say the victim had the life squeezed out of him slowly over an hour or so. Exactly when the process started and ended will be an interesting puzzle. I'll let you know when I've got an estimate." She shook her head. "Hell of a cold way to kill somebody."

I thought about the little gruesome touch the killer added to the Hawthorne hanging, thumbtacking the note to the judge's front. That was cold too.

David whispered behind his hand. "Are you ready to go? I've got enough shots, and Sloane's beginning to look at us funny."

"Yes. I want to beat it back to the paper and file the story."

Chapter Thirteen

IT WAS DARK WHEN I climbed the steps to my apartment. The corner of a white envelope sticking out of my mailbox caught my eye. I hardly ever get mail. Utilities are included in my rent, and I have no family to send letters or birthday cards and the like. I don't mean to sound sorry for myself. David and Gene are like family, but if they want to communicate with me, they simply yell up the stairs.

The envelope had my name in red crayon with no postage or return address. Just like the one the killer left me at the *Gazette* front desk. Whoever it was had hand delivered it right to my front door. I ran inside the brownstone and banged on Gene and David's apartment. David answered. "Hey, baybee." He backed up a step. "What's wrong? Your face is as white as a sheet."

I held up the envelope. "Another letter. I think it's from the killer. He delivered it here. The killer was right here."

"Eugene, turn down that TV." He pulled me inside.

I started ripping the envelope open. Gene scooted over to make room for me on the couch. "Shouldn't you be careful not to mess up fingerprints or something?" He ran across the room, rummaged in a drawer, and came back with woolen mittens. "These are all I could find."

I put on the mittens and tore open the envelope. Inside was another Halloween card. On the front, the silhouette of a witch on a broomstick flew across a huge blood-red orb. Inside the message said, "Beware the Blood Wolf Moon."

There was a letter. I read it out loud.

DEAR ELEANOR,

I TOLD YOU THERE WOULD BE MORE TO COME. I'M GLAD YOUR EDITOR HAS SEEN THE LIGHT AND GIVEN YOU THE SOLO BYLINE FOR MY STORY. I SUSPECT THE PAPER WILL EXPERIENCE

AN INCREASE IN CIRCULATION AS A RESULT OF MR. PUTNAM'S
FAME. THE INCREASE IN READERSHIP WILL BENEFIT ALL OF US.
PEOPLE NEED TO HEAR MY MESSAGE, THAT SINS ECHO THROUGH
THE GENERATIONS AND PAYMENT FINALLY COMES DUE. I AM
MERELY THE AGENT, AND YOU ARE THE SCRIBE.

BY NOW YOUNG MR. PUTNAM WILL HAVE BEEN
DISCOVERED. YOU MIGHT SAY HE PAID A HEAVY PRICE...

David interrupted me. "Did he mean that as a cruel pun?
Heartless!"

HIS FATE IS AN ESSENTIAL PART OF THE PLAN TO SETTLE THE
DEBT. I WISH YOU COULD HAVE BEEN WITH ME TO SEE IT
FIRSTHAND.

Bile rose in my throat. "What does he mean by that? He
considers me an accomplice?"
I went back to reading.

I'LL PAINT YOU A WORD PICTURE. THINGS WENT QUITE
SMOOTHLY THIS TIME. I WAS BETTER PREPARED THAN WITH THE
JUDGE. I SPENT SEVERAL WEEKS TRACKING TOMMY'S MOVES.
HE'S A MAN OF HABITS. HE VISITS THE CONSTRUCTION SITE
EVERY NIGHT AT THE SAME TIME. ALL THE MATERIALS I NEEDED
WERE AT HAND. I SIMPLY HID IN THE SHADOWS UNTIL I HEARD
THE ELEVATOR. OF COURSE, THERE COULD HAVE BEEN SOMEONE
WITH HIM, IN WHICH CASE I WOULD HAVE ABORTED AND
POSTPONED, BUT LUCKY FOR ME HE WAS ALONE.

WHEN HE TURNED HIS BACK TO CHECK SOME BLUEPRINTS, I
LUNGED AND INJECTED THE ANESTHETIC INTO HIS NECK. HE
DROPPED WHERE HE STOOD. I ROLLED HIM OVER, PLACED THE
NOTE ON HIS CHEST, AND BEGAN STACKING THE CINDER BLOCKS.
I PILED ON ENOUGH WEIGHT TO PIN HIM FIRMLY, THEN I
INJECTED THE WAKE-UP SHOT. HIS EYES POPPED OPEN AND, FOR
A MOMENT, HE WAS INCREDULOUS. HE COULDN'T BELIEVE
SOMETHING BAD WAS HAPPENING TO HIM. HE SAID, "YOU'VE

GOT TO BE KIDDING. DO YOU KNOW WHO I AM?" I ASSURED HIM I KNEW VERY WELL WHO HE WAS. THAT WAS THE POINT.

THEN HE BECAME ANGRY. HE STRUGGLED AND SWORE AND THREATENED. I KNEW HE WAS IN NO POSITION TO DELIVER ON ANY THREATS, BUT I MUST ADMIT, HE HAS...HAD...QUITE A COMMANDING PRESENCE, AND HE'S YOUNG AND FIT, OF COURSE. TO TELL THE TRUTH, I'M NOT AS YOUNG AS I USED TO BE, AND I HAD TO GIVE MYSELF A LITTLE TALKING-TO TO KEEP PILING ON THE BLOCKS.

Gene spoke up. "There's a clue. He's not a young person."

THEN HE STARTED BARGAINING. BEING THE DEALMAKER HE IS, THIS CALMED HIM DOWN. HE WAS CONFIDENT HE COULD FIND MY PRICE. HE OFFERED ME A MILLION DOLLARS, TWO MILLION, TEN MILLION. BUT MONEY MEANS NOTHING TO ME. I QUOTED THE BIBLE VERSE TO HIM, "PREPARE SLAUGHTER FOR HIS CHILDREN FOR THE INIQUITY OF THEIR FATHERS; THAT THEY DO NOT RISE, NOR POSSESS THE LAND, NOR FILL THE FACE OF THE WORLD WITH CITIES."

HE STARTED TO CRY. HE TALKED ABOUT HIS WIFE AND HIS TWO SONS, AND HOW THEY DEPEND ON HIM FOR EVERYTHING. HE WAS STRUGGLING TO SPEAK, AND HIS SOBBING DIDN'T MAKE BREATHING ANY EASIER. AFTER A WHILE, HE SEEMED TO ACCEPT THE INEVITABLE. HE WAS QUIET FOR SEVERAL MINUTES, AND I THOUGHT IT WAS OVER. BUT HE SURPRISED ME. AFTER ONE FINAL FUTILE STRUGGLE, HE SAID HIS LAST WORDS: "MORE WEIGHT."

David, Gene, and I said "Ugh" in unison.

YOU'RE WORKING WITH THE POLICE. THE YOUNG WOMAN OFFICER IS QUITE ATTRACTIVE, ISN'T SHE? I SUPPOSE IT'S TO BE EXPECTED THAT YOU WOULD COLLABORATE WITH THE AUTHORITIES, BUT I WOULD BE VERY DISAPPOINTED IF YOU USED OUR RELATIONSHIP TO HELP THEM FIND ME AND INTERRUPT MY

PROGRESS. I WON'T WORRY ABOUT THAT NOW. I NEED TO
FOCUS ON THE NEXT STEP.

I LOOK FORWARD TO YOUR NEWSPAPER ARTICLE ABOUT MR.
PUTNAM. UNTIL NEXT TIME...

The letter was unsigned except for the same symbol at the
bottom, the Solar Cross with the red dot between ten and eleven
on the circle, a little closer now to the eleven. I held the page so
David could see. "Walt Smith says it's a witches' symbol."

David nodded. "It's the same as with Judge Hawthorne.
Aren't the police trying to chase this stuff down?"

"They are, but Sloane is sticking with his theory that the killer
is trying to throw the police off the scent with the sins of the
father business. They have a primary suspect who was sentenced
to prison and just got out on parole, and he has Detective Carr
chasing down other suspects who might hold a grudge directly
against the victims, not anything to do with their fathers." I slid off
the couch and started for the door. "I'm going to call Detective
Carr and tell her about this letter."

David held up his finger. "Just a minute. The part about you
working with the police sounds like a threat. He said he'd be very
disappointed. Aren't you afraid he might take it further than being
disappointed? I don't like his implication. He might try harming
you."

Gene went to the windows and peered down at the street.
"David's right. The guy knows where you live, and he knows
you're working with Detective Carr. He's got to be following you.
He might be out there in the dark right now."

David walked across the room and came back holding a small
black leather case. He unzipped it. Inside was a pistol.

"A gun? Is it loaded?"

"I don't think so. I've never had it out of the case. My grandpa
gave the thing to me when I moved. He said he wouldn't let me
come up North without protection. I think you'll find bullets in the
side pocket."

I hesitated. I knew nothing about guns. Me with a weapon could be more dangerous than the killer's threats.

David held it out. "Just take it. You don't have to load it."

"I guess I might use it to scare somebody." I took the case. "I've got to call Carr about the letter."

In my apartment, I looked around for a place to hide the gun. I stretched on tiptoes and stashed the case above the kitchen cabinet. I dialed Christine at the Barbizon Hotel. The front desk rang her room, and she answered on the first ring. "Carr speaking."

"Christine, Butch. I got another letter, this time about the Putnam murder." I struggled to control my shaky voice. "The killer delivered it to my apartment."

"Okay." She picked up the alarm in my tone. "Take a deep breath and tell me exactly what happened. Did you see anyone suspicious around your apartment?"

"No, I just got home from work. I didn't see anyone. The envelope was sticking out of my mailbox. No postage and no return address. It's another Halloween card and a note written in the same red crayon. I can read it to you."

"Can you bring it to my hotel now? The corner of Lexington and Sixty-Third."

"I know the place. I'll be right there." I grabbed the envelope and ran down the stairs and out the front door to hail a cab.

Traffic was light at that time of night. The taxi stopped in front of the twenty-three-story, salmon-colored brick hotel. A green awning over the glass front doors spelled "The Barbizon" in fancy script. A doorman rushed to help me from the car. Christine was waiting in the lobby.

I looked around the space. "Pretty swanky."

"It was once. If you look closely, you'll notice the famous Barbizon has lost some luster. It's fine for my purposes. The neighborhood's good, and there's a coffee shop off the lobby for meals and a pool in the basement for workouts."

"A pool. Nice." I'm not a swimmer. When most people were learning to swim, I was honing my skating skills for my carhop job at the Dairy Queen. To tell the truth, I'm a little afraid of water.

"Yes, best of all, no one ever goes down there. The girls who live here are not the exercise type, so I have the pool to myself. I mainly just sleep here anyway." She looked at the envelope in my hand. "Is that the letter?"

I nodded. "Guess I've messed up the fingerprints. I grabbed it and ran out of the apartment without thinking."

"Don't worry. If it's like last time, the killer wore gloves." She gestured across the lobby. "Let's go in the coffee shop. I haven't eaten yet."

"Come to think of it, I haven't either."

The café off the lobby was empty. A waitress popped her chewing gum and waved two menus toward the tables. "Take your pick, ladies."

We chose a booth by the front windows and ordered grilled cheese sandwiches and tomato soup.

I slid the envelope across the table. Christine shook out the Halloween card and the letter. She read the letter to herself. "The killer delivered it to your apartment?"

"Yes."

"Do you have any idea what this person's connection to you might be?"

"Not a clue. If you take him at his word, it's my reporting."

"Well, there's clearly a link with you that might help us. And it sounds like you're being followed."

"David and Gene said the same thing."

She picked up the card. "The Halloween cards seem out of left field, not much help beyond carrying along the witch theme. The letters have some possible leads. The description of injecting the victim with a drug. The Hawthorne tox report came back today. The killer anesthetized him with propofol. I'll bet we find the same substance in Putnam's system. You don't buy propofol off a drugstore shelf, and the manufacturers and retailers keep

85

close track of sales. We may be able to run down who bought the drug recently."

"Where are you with questioning Edwina K. Stone?"

"The prison paroled her to an Astoria halfway house. We'll send some uniforms out to bring her to the station for questioning and see if she has an alibi for the two murders. They are clearly connected. I'm combing through Stone's background, and I'll interview Tina, the second vic's wife, tomorrow. I think we'll find our answers where Judge Hawthorne and Tommy Putnam intersect."

"I know the Julia Rains lead turned out to be a bust, but now there's another note about sins of the father."

"Sloane figures the bit about the fathers is a red herring, a diversion from a revenge motive against the judge and the billionaire."

"What do you think?"

She tucked the curl behind her ear. "Hawthorne and Putnam are Sloane's cases. He calls the shots. We're focused on Edwina K. Stone right now."

"How do I convince him to open up to the possibility that these murders are revenge for acts by the fathers?"

"Bring us some evidence that pans out."

"Not like Julia Rains."

"Exactly."

The waitress set our soup and sandwiches in front of us. "Can I get you gals anything else?"

We said, "No thanks" in unison.

She stood back with her hands on her hips. "Well, I'll leave the two of you to yourselves." She gave me a big wink.

Was the waitress picking up on something like David did? Was I releasing pheromones or something? Was my attraction as transparent to Christine as it seemed to others? A flush started in my solar plexus and moved up my neck.

I took a bite of sandwich and searched for something to say. "So, what motivated you to leave Buffalo and come to NYPD?"

She put down her soup spoon and looked out the window. It had started raining. The window glass muted the rhythmic swish of the tires of passing cars. "More money, greater promotion opportunities." Her voice trailed off like she had more to say but thought better of it. She picked up her spoon again. "Mostly I needed a change of scenery."

"I've never been to Buffalo, but I suspect you certainly got a change of scenery coming to New York City."

"Yes, the biggest difference is there's never a downtime. I'm having trouble sleeping because of the constant buzz of activity in the street. I keep wondering what I'm missing."

"As they say, the city that never sleeps. It takes getting used to. In Wilmington, they roll up the sidewalks at dark."

"That's where you're from?"

"Yes, Wilmington. The one in North Carolina."

"You still have family there."

She said it like a statement instead of a question. Not surprising she'd assume I have relatives in North Carolina, given my age and my accent. When I tell people about Sisters of the Merciful Heart, they react with pity or curiosity. I dreaded either reaction from Christine. I took a deep breath. "I grew up in an orphanage."

Her response was neither of the usual. She nodded. "That explains it."

"Explains what?"

"Why you're so self-reliant."

I stopped a spoonful of soup halfway to my mouth. "That's a good thing, right?"

Before she answered, Christine looked deeply into my eyes and held my gaze. Have you ever noticed how you go through life rarely ever looking directly into someone's eyes? Sister Marie Madeline used to hold my face in her hands and look deeply into my eyes and tell me how smart I was and never mind the other girls teasing me about my size. She'd say "Don't pay any attention to them. You're special, and you'll do special things in this world. You'll make your own way."

A tiny smile lifted the corners of Christine's mouth. "It's a very good thing."

We are both fast eaters, Christine and I. We finished our soups and sandwiches, and she signaled the waitress for the check. "Are you in a rush? How about a walk in the city that never sleeps?"

"Sounds good."

I reached for the letter and card. Christine covered my hand with hers. "Don't print it. There are details in the letter only the killer will know. They might help us identify suspects."

"I can't promise that, Christine. It's my job."

"I know, and I'm trying to do my job too. At least wait until we get the tox screen on Putnam and question Edwina Stone."

"I'll try, but I can't promise. My city editor is giving me a shot at the crime beat, and it's super important I don't let him down."

Christine borrowed an oversized black umbrella from the bellman at the front door. "Okay with you if we share the umbrella? We can talk easier that way." We paused just outside the hotel door under the green awning. She pointed south down Lexington. "Look at the moon. It's blood red, just like on the Halloween card. Like a big cherry stuck on the top of the Chrysler Building."

Christine held the umbrella between us and put her arm around my shoulders, pulling me close to her side. Sometimes it feels like you fit perfectly next to someone. That's how it felt. I glanced at her to see if she noticed it too. She still had that little smile on her lips.

We crossed the street and headed west on 63rd toward the park. The rain kept up a steady thrumming on the umbrella's taut fabric. Even at the late hour, the sidewalk was full of families wearing heavy coats and carrying blankets and coolers.

Christine navigated us around a couple with three little kids. "Where's everybody going at this hour in this weather?"

"They're headed across the park to line up for the Macy's Thanksgiving Day Parade. They'll camp out on the street to guarantee a good viewing spot. You do know tomorrow is Thanksgiving, right?"

"Of course, but it'll be just another day for me."

"You don't have family to go to for Thanksgiving dinner?"

"All in Massachusetts, an hour north of Boston. And I'm not exactly close with them. I'll probably go into the precinct after I meet with Tina Putnam and clear the decks for next week. Things are moving too slowly for my taste, with the holidays and all. We shouldn't be wasting any time with a killer on the loose. There's the Stone interview, and I'm starting the search for ex-employees and contractors who might have a grudge against Putnam." She glanced at me. "You're thinking the job doesn't sound like the exciting movie version of a big-city detective's life. You're right, but I love everything about it. Even slogging through paperwork."

"I wasn't thinking that. Certainly you love your job. I love mine too. I wasn't thinking about our jobs. The truth is, I was plotting a way to convince you to skip work and come to dinner with me at David and Gene's. Gene's cooking turkey and all the trimmings, and David's making his grandma's Karo pecan pie."

"What's Karo pecan pie?" She pronounced it "pee-can," like a Yankee.

"It's a Southern thing, too complicated to explain, even if I had the first idea how to make a pie. But you'll have to trust me, Karo pecan pie is delicious. David and I will cover the parade for the paper in the morning. When are you interviewing Tina Putnam?"

"Tomorrow morning in their apartment."

"You could come to David and Gene's around four o'clock."

"Are you sure it's all right with David and Gene?"

"Certainly. Gene always makes way too much food. Only one condition. You have to agree to play Clue after dinner. Gene will think competing against an honest-to-goodness detective is hilarious. And, forewarned, he always wins the game."

"I agree to the condition. What can I bring? It will have to come from the deli. No cooking at the Barbizon, even if I could cook, which I can't."

"Just bring some wine."

"Good. See you tomorrow at four. Thank you." She squeezed my shoulder, and my solar plexus buzzed again.

* * * *

After Thanksgiving dinner, Gene won the Clue game, as I predicted. Colonel Mustard did it with the candlestick in the conservatory. Gene, the aspiring Sherlock Holmes, flatly refused to let Christine and me do the dishes. David sat on the stoop and watched as I walked Christine to the corner to hail a cab. David was worried about the killer stalking me.

Christine and I stopped in the circle of light under a streetlamp. "Thank you for inviting me. David and Gene are wonderful. You're lucky to have them in your life. Their beautiful apartment motivates me to start thinking seriously about finding a place of my own. And as you promised, the Karo pecan pie was incredible."

She waved at David and then turned back to me. "I didn't want to mention it in front of your friends, but I had a major development in my interview with Tina Putnam. She ID'd Edwina's mug shot. Tina used a temp agency maid for a few days several years ago. Guess who? Edwina. Tina called the agency and got Edwina fired because she came to work stoned. Edwina did not leave quietly. Tommy Putnam had to physically throw her out of their apartment. Edwina was pretty graphic about how she would retaliate. Near as I can tell, only a few days later she was arrested in Times Square for selling heroin."

"Can I report on this?"

"Hold off till we talk with Edwina."

"I'll try."

"Well." She opened her arms and wrapped me in a long embrace. I breathed in the clean smell of her hair. If I asked her to spend the night, would she say yes?

I missed my moment. A taxi pulled to the curb, and I watched till the taillights disappeared down Seventh Avenue. I walked back to our building, and David scooted over and patted the stone step beside him. "Let's sit here a minute, darlin', and enjoy the night air." He wrapped one side of his jacket around my shoulders, pulled me in tight, and pointed at the sky. "You can almost make out some stars. The night sky is one thing I miss about home. In Mississippi, you can see a million stars, like tiny diamonds against black velvet. As a kid, I tried to photograph the sky over Greenwood, but pictures never did it justice."

Music drifted from the front window of their apartment, Etta James singing "At Last." David hummed along. "Our song. We've about worn a hole in the record."

"Tell me again about how you and Gene got together. The story always makes me feel warm and fuzzy...and hopeful I might have a relationship like yours someday."

"I went to dinner in the Village with some friends, and Gene came to the same restaurant with a group. A fellow in my party knew one in his, and we wound up all sitting together at a big round table." He smiled at the memory. "Gene has a great laugh."

"Yes, he does."

"He thought I was hilarious that night, which won my heart right away, of course. You could hear him guffaw all over the restaurant. When he left, he handed me a blank deposit slip from the back of his checkbook printed with his phone number and address. I called him the next day, and the rest is history." He glanced at me. "I expected Christine might stay all night with you."

"I wanted her to."

"Did you ask her?"

"No."

He shook his head. "I'll never understand gay women. If you wanted her to stay, why didn't you just let her know?"

A wind gust blew leaves along the sidewalk, and I shivered a little. "The timing doesn't seem right. It's complicated right now. We're in danger of being on opposite sides of the Hawthorne and Putnam cases. She's asked me to hold off reporting about the second letter and other leads they've got."

"Are you going to do that?"

"I honestly don't know how I can."

"Sounds to me like you need to find a way to get on the same side with her."

"How would I get on the same side? I can't let the cops dictate what I report."

"Help her solve the cases."

"I'm trying. I found some intriguing information about Judge Hawthorne's father. He did something that might lead a person to hold a grudge against him, but it turned out to be a dead end. Now there's Tommy Putnam's murder. The connection between Hawthorne and Putnam's fathers must be important, but I haven't found it yet."

"My money's on you to find the answer, baybee. You never give up."

Chapter Fourteen

DUKE STOMPED OUT OF his office. He had his hat on, pushed back on his head with the brim turned up in front. The hat is never a good sign. It doesn't mean he's going somewhere. It's like a security blanket. Somehow wearing a hat indoors makes him feel more in control. "Butch, in my office."

I grabbed a pencil and pad and followed him.

He dropped into his chair. "Where are you with The Avenger murders?"

We had started calling the killer The Avenger around the newsroom because of the quotes from the Bible and allusions to payback in the notes left on the bodies.

I glanced at the wooden straight chair in front of the city editor's desk, wondering if I should sit down or just stand. I decided to sit.

He got up and paced. "Circulation's down. We had a good pop when you got the letter about Hawthorne, but it's tailing off. The publisher's asking."

I pictured the Putnam letter waiting in the top drawer of my desk. If not for Christine's request, I would be writing it up for the paper's next edition.

He sat back down. "Where are the cops with the case? Aren't you tight with the lady cop, Detective What's-Her-Name?"

"Detective Carr. They have a suspect, a woman who was paroled from Bedford Hills two weeks before the judge's murder. They're bringing her in for questioning. They're pretty sure the two murders are connected."

"Did you say their suspect is female? Boy, that would make a sensational story. Whatever, you need to get an angle on it and give me something. Maybe Harry can help."

I gave him a thumbs-up. "Right, chief. You can count on me."

I sat down at my desk and chewed on a hangnail. Duke hadn't exactly ordered me to ask Harry for help. I could, but wouldn't bringing Harry back be admitting I couldn't handle a crime assignment? Walt Smith walked by, returning from one of his many trips to the men's room. He appeared to be losing weight, but not healthy weight loss. His face looked a little gaunt.

He paused in front of my desk. "Why so pensive, Eleanor?"

I took the envelope out of my desk drawer and shook out the letter. "It's this letter from The Avenger." I handed it to him. "What about the Bible quote?"

Walt sat down at his desk and put on his reading glasses. He scanned the letter and handed it back. "The words of the eighth-century BC prophet Isaiah to the Jews in captivity in Babylon. He foresaw the time they would revolt, vanquish their captors, and destroy the great cities the tyrants had built to glorify themselves. He specifically urged God's chosen people to slaughter the captors' children. He gave two reasons: first, as retribution for their fathers' sins, and second, so the children couldn't rise up and repeat them."

"What do you think the quote means in connection with The Avenger murders?"

Walt shrugged. "It seems consistent with the first letter. The murder victims are paying for the sins of their fathers, and The Avenger has chosen you as his partner. He wants you to get out a message. I'd say that's quite a compliment to your journalistic skills."

I took the letter back. The partner of a cold-blooded killer? "Thanks, Walt. I need Duke to leave me on this story. If I'm the scribe like the letter says, I better get busy finding an angle."

I took the elevator back to the morgue. *Advance Obits* listed Tommy Putnam's father as Thomas Putnam, Senior, and Scotty found his clipping file. The Putnam, Senior folder was different from Professor Hawthorn's slim file. It was four inches thick. I started at the back with the earliest clippings and worked my way forward in time.

Flipping through the file was like reading a picture book starring a slum landlord. The first story, dated 1927, showed Putnam, Senior marching in a Ku Klux Klan parade down Fifth Avenue. Article after article followed, reporting run-ins with the

New York Attorney General, the Manhattan District Attorney, and the Federal Housing Authority. The stories detailed deplorable conditions in his lower Manhattan, Brooklyn, and Queens apartment buildings. In one case, a judge ordered the elder Putnam to live for a month in a rundown building so he could experience plumbing problems and vermin infestations with his tenants. No indication that experience changed his business practices.

Among the articles covering his legal problems were photos of Putnam in a tuxedo and his wives in cocktail dresses, hobnobbing with the mayor and other elected officials and celebrities at various charity functions. Having money buys you access to powerful people in this city, no matter how despicable your methods for making money are.

The photos showed two different wives over time. In the early years, Mrs. Putnam was a rather dowdy lady about Putnam's age. Sometime in the early 1940s, a new model replaced dowdy Mrs. Putnam. The second Mrs. Putnam looked like a cross between Rita Hayworth and Lana Turner, red-haired and full-figured.

Another long article bore the headline, "Developer Key Witness in Coogan Bribery Trial." In exchange for immunity, Putnam, Senior testified in the trial of the Queens borough president, James J. Coogan, charged with accepting roughly $5,000 in apartment renovations from his longtime friend. Guess who the friend was? Putnam, Senior. Heading the article was a photo of Putnam leaving a courthouse surrounded by police and lawyer types. The story's byline was Walt Smith. That was lucky. Walt could fill me in on the case. Maybe James J. Coogan would have a motive for murder.

The last clipping showed Putnam, Senior, withered from the cancer that finally took him, shaking his son's hand as the father formally turned over the reins of The Putnam Company.

The elder Putnam had plenty of sins, but the file held no clues about a connection between Judge Hawthorne and Tommy.

I returned the file to Scotty, who was busy clipping articles from the most recent edition of the paper. "Any luck?"

"Lots of potential sins to check out. No obvious connection with the Hawthorne family yet. I need to buy time by getting something in type or Duke is going to take me off the story and give it back to Harry."

I hurried up to the newsroom to ask Walt about the Queens bribery case. He wasn't at his desk. Maybe Duke was right about getting advice from Harry. Maybe he could help me decide how to handle Christine's insistence I not report on the Putnam letter. I grabbed the letter and Halloween card out of my desk drawer and walked across the newsroom to Harry's desk. He was pounding away on his typewriter in his shirtsleeves with a cigarette hanging from his lips. His blockbuster exposé series about Carlo Gambino, boss of the Gambino crime family, was causing everyone in New York City to sit up and take notice. He was busy. I started to turn away and head back to my desk when he glanced up. "Butch. What can I do for you?"

"You're busy."

"Yeah. I've got an FBI buddy who tipped me off about a raid tomorrow night on a Gambino warehouse in Brooklyn. Thought I'd get a jump on the story so I can scoop the *Times* once the plan is out in the open."

"You know about the planned raid, but you're holding off reporting it till it happens? That's sort of what I wanted to talk to you about. A similar situation." I handed him the letter and card. "The Avenger hand delivered this to my apartment."

Harry blew out a whistle.

"Yeah. I showed it to Detective Carr, and she's asked me to hold off writing the story because there are some details in the letter that might help them catch the killer. That doesn't seem right to me, but I'm not sure what to do."

"Duke know about this?"

I shook my head. "Not yet."

The veteran reporter pushed his chair back and stretched. "Get your coat and let's go for a walk. I could use a break."

In the street, the sun was shining, but an icy wind whipped around the corner of the *Gazette* building and lifted the hems of our coats. Harry glanced down at me. "You okay, or do you want to duck into a coffee shop?"

"I'm okay."

"Good. The cold clears the mind."

We headed south, dodging delivery guys pushing loaded hand trucks from their double-parked vans and bundled-up women with net bags full of the evening's groceries. Harry ambled along with his hands in his pockets. He seemed in no rush to answer my question about The Avenger's letter. I wanted him to tell me what to do about Christine's insistence I hold off on reporting it. Well, I didn't exactly want him to tell me what to do. I wanted him to tell me what he would do in my place. A subtle but important difference in my view.

"So. You're holding up reporting about the FBI raid on the Gambinos even though your buddy tipped you off. Detective Carr is asking me to hold up reporting on The Avenger's letter. Isn't it the same thing? If you were in my place, would you do what she's asking?"

Harry stopped to light a cigarette, cupping his hand around the match to shield it from the wind. "Here's how I've always thought about it. It's not my job to catch or prosecute criminals. That's for the cops and the courts. My job is to find the important truth, verify it, and report it to my readers. My FBI raid hasn't happened yet. The important thing for my readers to know is what results from the raid, not that there's going to be one. If I tip the Gambinos off, the raid very likely won't happen."

"So you're saying if the facts are important to our readers, I should report them."

"If I were in your place, I'd do my job and let Detective Carr do hers."

I grabbed Harry and hugged him. "You're right. Thanks, Harry."

I left him in the street, ran back up to my typewriter, and spooled a sheet of paper in. I hesitated over the keys. I would write the story, but I could also give Christine a heads-up before she read it in the paper. I dialed her direct number, and she answered on the first ring. "Detective Carr."

"Christine, it's Butch. I've held off writing about the letter like you asked for as long as I can."

Silence on the other end. She blew out a breath. "We're stalled with the investigation. Stone is missing from the halfway house in Astoria. She hasn't been seen for two weeks."

"How was NYPD in the dark about that?"

"It's an example of the right hand not knowing what the left hand is doing. Probation reported it, but the paperwork was still wending its way through the system. We've put out an APB. We'll get her eventually, but in the meantime we're stuck. We've got your letters and the notes on the bodies. The tox screen on Tommy came in. It's propofol, same as Hawthorne. We've got physical evidence that links the two murders but no motive."

I grabbed my notebook. "Are we on the record?"

She blew another breath. "Yes. Maybe someone will read your story and call in a lead on the propofol. It's sold almost exclusively to hospitals, but there are sixty-three of those in Manhattan alone, not to mention Long Island and New Jersey. And who knows how well the hospitals keep track of their supply. I've started making calls already."

"You sound beat."

"I didn't rest well last night. Remember, 'the city that never sleeps.' But mostly I sound this way because I'm disappointed we don't have our suspect."

"Let me get busy and write the story and rustle you up some public reaction." I finished the article with details from The Avenger's second letter. Duke was on the phone in his office. I dropped the letter and the story in his inbox and went back to my desk and waited. I crossed my fingers he'd be so jazzed about letter number two, he wouldn't ask how and when I got it. I wasn't looking forward to explaining the complicated interaction Christine and I had.

Duke motioned me into his office. As I hoped, he was too excited to ask for details. "Sensational, Butch. This leads in the morning edition. I suppose you better messenger the letter over to Sloane right away. He can't be too mad. This bit about the propofol should stir up some leads from the public. Good work, kiddo."

I went back to my desk and read over my notes from the Putnam, Senior clippings file. I underlined three points for follow-up. First, the deplorable conditions in rental units owned by The Putnam Company. Maybe a tenant decided to redress some grievances against Putnam by killing his son. Second, the abrupt change from dowdy Mrs. Putnam to movie star Mrs. Putnam. Third, the James J. Coogan scandal. The Coogan story with Walt's byline. He'd be the best source for information on the trial and conviction of the Queens borough president. I checked with Duke, and he told me Walt called in sick that morning. I'd have to catch him the next day if he was back at his desk. In the meantime, who could shed light on the first two questions?

A picture of the foreman at the Putnam murder scene flashed in my mind. I flipped back through the pages of my notes from that morning and found the foreman's name, Mirelli. *Started working with Senior. Been with Junior since he took over the company.* He might have information about both the code violations and the two wives.

Chapter Fifteen

EARLY THE NEXT MORNING, I stood on the street in front of 666 Fifth Avenue, the building where Tommy was killed. Two construction cranes loomed over the top of the high-rise like a pair of giant praying mantises. The steel girders framing the building clanged with strikes from rivet guns. Blooms of sparks from welders' torches lit up the structure like July Fourth. Work continued despite the owner's grizzly death on the top floor.

A green canvas fence screened the construction site from the sidewalk. I followed it around the corner, waited while a dump truck exited an open gate, and slipped inside. The truck driver gave me a curious look, then shrugged as if to say, *Not my job,* and drove on.

I hailed the closest workman, yelling over the racket. "The boss, Mr. Mirelli?"

He pointed up. I was in for another scary construction elevator ride. I stepped into the empty elevator and looked for any clues on how to run the thing. No buttons with floor numbers. No START and STOP. Just an unlabeled lever. I wished I'd paid better attention the first time to how to operate the elevator. Should I risk it or give up? *How bad do you want this, Tracy?* I was about to shut the metal door and pull the lever to start the thing when Mirelli himself stepped onto the elevator.

I stuck out my hand, forgetting the hook. "Butch Tracy." It was an awkward moment for me, but not for Mirelli. He was used to it. He gave me a curt nod.

"Mr. Mirelli, you may not remember me. I came with the police the morning you found Mr. Putnam's body." That was not technically a lie. I said I came with the cops, not that I was a cop, but I decided I'd better clarify. "I'm with the *Gazette*. Is there someplace we can talk? We're trying to find who might have done such a terrible thing."

He looked at his watch. "I've already told the detectives everything I know."

"Right, and the police are pursuing all leads. I just want to follow up on some background you might have about Tommy Putnam's father."

He pulled the elevator door closed. "I can spare a few minutes. It's quieter up top."

On the fifteenth floor, all signs of the murder were gone. A makeshift worktable, a piece of plywood laid across two sawhorses, stood where The Avenger squeezed the life from Tommy. Mirelli moved a stack of blueprints aside and nodded toward a metal folding chair. He looked at his watch again. "How can I help you?"

"You told Detective Sloane you worked for Mr. Putnam, Senior before Tommy took over the company."

"I started working for Mr. Putnam in 1938 when I was still in high school, before The Putnam Company existed. He owned three or four apartment buildings in Queens, and my family lived in one."

"I've read newspaper reports about conditions in those buildings. Did your family have rats and leaky plumbing?"

Mirelli didn't respond right away. Something changed in his eyes. His gaze hardened, and he leaned across the table toward me. The move wasn't exactly menacing, but I was suddenly super aware of how isolated the two of us were at the top of that building where Tommy Putnam died. Maybe I should start carrying David's gun around. "What exactly do you want to know about Mr. Putnam?"

"You saw the note the killer left on Tommy's body. He claims Tommy died as repayment for a debt his father owed. I'm trying to discover what that debt is and how it could relate to another murder, maybe by the same killer."

"So, you're looking for dirt on Mr. Putnam."

"I'm not looking for dirt on Thomas Putnam, Mr. Mirelli. Just some connection with clues to how the police might solve two murders and prevent any more."

He settled back in his seat. "My father left us when I was young and my sister was a baby. Mama worked sixteen hours a day, seven days a week to put food on the table and a roof over our heads. She didn't have the time or energy to keep me on track, and I fell in with a rough crowd. Mr. Putnam noticed me hanging around the neighborhood and paid me to do errands and small jobs around his rentals and construction sites. He took me under his wing. He and the first Mrs. Putnam didn't have any children."

"So you became sort of a son to him."

"I wouldn't go that far. I'm just saying his help kept me in school. Mr. Putnam talked about pulling some strings and getting me into a plumbing apprenticeship after high school, but when I was in tenth grade, this happened." He held up his right arm and studied the hook like it belonged to someone else.

"How did you lose your arm?"

"Girder fell on it."

"You were working on a construction site at that age? Weren't there laws against that?"

"Mr. Putnam wasn't much of one for following bureaucratic laws."

I nodded. His file in the *Gazette* morgue illustrated that point well.

"After the accident, he gave me a job as a super at one of his buildings and let my mother and sister and me live there free in exchange. It was a generous act for my family."

Or Putnam may have felt guilty about the arm. Or he may have been trying to avoid a lawsuit.

Mirelli's left thumb stroked the hook's shiny metal. "I finished high school and went to junior college and took the contractor's license exam. By the time I got my license, Mr. Putnam owned hundreds of housing units in Queens, Brooklyn, and lower Manhattan. I went to work for the company full time. Been working for the Putnams ever since."

Mirelli was starting to look like another dead end. I tried a different tack. "I've read newspaper accounts of deplorable conditions in Putnam's buildings. Plumbing problems and vermin."

Mirelli snorted. "Most of his renters would have lived on the street with no plumbing at all without his buildings. You can put his troubles with the city and state and Feds down to a bunch of bureaucrats and politicians threatened by Mr. Putnam's success."

"Can you think of anyone who would hold enough of a grudge against Putnam to murder his son, maybe someone angry about living conditions in his buildings or a disgruntled subcontractor?"

Mirelli shook his head. He looked at his watch again.

"You mentioned Mr. Putnam's first wife. What happened to her?"

"She passed away. Cancer. Mr. Putnam remarried, and they had a baby, Tommy."

So much for any dreams Mirelli might have harbored of being the rich man's son he never had. "And he grew up to take over the company."

"He had the business in his blood."

"By all the signs, Tommy was very successful. It must have been a challenge taking orders from such a young guy. He was very hands-on."

The steely look came back in Mirelli's eyes. "It's his company, and he worked hard." He pushed his chair back. "Is there anything else? I need to check on some things."

"Just one more question. Does the name Dr. Jackson Bradford Hawthorne ring any bells in connection with Mr. Putnam, Senior? He was a professor at Columbia."

He shook his head. "What kind of a professor?"

"English Literature."

"That doesn't sound like Mr. Putnam, but Columbia was always after him for money, like most of the charities in town. They used to invite him and his wife to all the fancy fundraiser parties. I never heard him mention a Professor Hawthorne."

I put one of my cards in front of him. "If anything else occurs to you, Mr. Mirelli, please call me at the paper."

He didn't pick up the card or even look at it. He stood and headed for the elevator with me trailing behind.

* * * *

At the *Gazette*, I found Walt in the break room eating a pastrami sandwich. "Walt, glad you're better. Say, you caught the story way back when about the Queens borough president's bribery trial." I looked at my notes. "James J. Coogan. The star witness against him was Thomas Putnam, father of our number two murder victim."

Walt stuffed the end of the sandwich into his mouth and held up a finger until he chewed and swallowed and dabbed his lips with a paper napkin. "A modern-day Greek tragedy, full of hubris, ambition, and betrayal. Coogan was a rising star in Democratic politics. He was elected to two terms as Queens borough president. With his charisma and influence in the mayor's office, everyone expected his next chapter would be state or national politics, Congress, or even the governor's office.

"Whether he overstepped himself, or the establishment wanted to take him down a peg is unknown, but he got caught in a bribery scandal. A developer did some work in Coogan's apartment at the same time he was bidding on a lucrative city contract. Coogan swore he meant to pay for the work, but the developer testified against him in court."

"Thomas Putnam was the developer."

"Yes."

"Where is Coogan now?"

He shook his head. "No idea. He served a few months in jail and disappeared from public life, as far as I know. Maybe there's something more about his recent whereabouts in the clippings morgue."

"Good idea. Thanks, Walt." I pushed back the chair.

"Hold on, Eleanor. Here's something interesting. As I recall, the judge in the Coogan case was one Honorable John Hawthorne."

"You're kidding!"

"Yes, I remember it quite clearly. Could be just a coincidence, of course."

"Thanks, Walt." I ran to the elevator. I needed to locate this Coogan guy. Down in the morgue, his clips file was full of articles about his successful political career and the bribery trial. I skimmed the reports about the trial for any mention of Judge Hawthorne but came up empty. There was a gap in time after Coogan's conviction. Then I found a clue to Coogan's whereabouts.

An article dated fifteen years after he went to jail detailed a US Attorney lawsuit against New York City Housing Authority. On behalf of a group of tenants, including James J. and Moira Coogan, the suit alleged the Authority violated health and safety regulations at a public apartment building on Amsterdam Avenue, exposing children to lead paint. The suit alleged the Authority trained its workers to deceive inspectors. They'd shut off buildings' water supplies during inspections to hide leaks, and they built false walls out of plywood to hide dilapidated rooms from inspectors. Housing Authority settled the lawsuit by admitting to the allegations and agreeing to spend an additional one billion dollars over the next four years on upkeep and maintenance. The byline on the article was Walt's again. Why hadn't he mentioned it? Must have slipped his mind. Maybe the veteran reporter was losing a step mentally.

The Coogans might still be living in the same building as when they participated in the lawsuit. At least the article gave me a place to start.

I took a cab to the public housing units on Amsterdam Avenue. If the Housing Authority spent a billion bucks, it certainly wasn't to spruce up the outside of the place. There must have been a grassy lawn around the building many years ago, but inattention and foot traffic had turned the ground into hard-packed dirt. Graffiti covered the building up to the level a guy could reach with a spray paint can. If Coogan lived here, it was quite a comedown for a man once headed for the governor's mansion. The wall of mailboxes by the front door was spray painted too, but I could just make out Coogan's name on a box, Apartment 550.

A middle-aged woman in orange polyester pedal pushers answered the door. In the background, *The Price Is Right* blared from the television.

I shouted over the noise. "Mrs. Coogan?" I handed her a card.

She studied it a moment, then leaned out and looked up and down the hallway, as though I must have brought other people with me. "I'm Moira Coogan."

"I'm looking for Mr. James Coogan. Is he in?"

"You won't find him here during the day. The old fool gets up every morning, puts on a suit and tie, and goes and sits in the park by himself." She glanced over her shoulder at the television, afraid she was missing something important on the quiz show. "You might find him by the lake." She shut the door in my face.

The area around the lake was deserted except for an occasional jogger and a man sitting alone on a bench. He was tossing bread crumbs from a paper bag to pigeons strutting back and forth on the path in front of him. I found a bench a few yards away to sit and watch. He didn't look like a killer, but what does a killer look like? Maybe when I've been crime reporting as long as Harry I'll be able to answer that question. He emptied the crumbs on the ground, wadded the paper bag into a ball, and leaned forward with his elbows on his knees. His lips moved like he was having a conversation with some invisible person sitting beside him.

I pushed up from the bench and walked toward him. "Mr. Coogan?"

He jerked upright. "Do I know you?" He was a slight man with sloping shoulders. The suit had been expensive in its day but bore the shine of years of wear and hung on his frame as though he'd lost a lot of weight at some point, I figured maybe in prison.

"No, sir. I'm a reporter from the *Gazette*. Can I talk to you?"

He looked up and down the path. "I was leaving."

"It won't take a minute. I just want to ask you about Thomas Putnam. His son was killed a few days ago, and the police think the murder might have something to do with Mr. Thomas Putnam." That was only a small lie. I had yet to convince Sloane the murders could be about the fathers. "You knew him, right? You might be able to help."

"Who did you say you are? You're the police?"

"No, sir. I'm a newspaper reporter." I sat on the bench next to him.

He looked around for where to put the empty paper bag and then stuck it in his coat pocket. "You say Putnam's son was murdered? Well, the apple doesn't fall far from the tree, so he probably deserved it."

"You were convicted of bribery and went to prison based on Thomas Putnam's testimony."

He nodded.

I opened my mouth to say, "How did that make you feel?" when Coogan saved me from asking a lame question.

"I came out of prison determined to clear my name. Putnam died of cancer before I could do that. He got out of this world owing me a debt. Maybe his son paid it. If you're looking for sympathy for the Putnam family, you won't find any here."

He rose abruptly, and the pigeons that had been hanging around scattered, their hopes of more handouts dashed.

"Just one more question, please, Mr. Coogan. Your trial was in Judge Hawthorne's court." I watched his face for a reaction to the judge's name.

He put his hands up as though to physically ward off any more questions. "There was no way I was going to get a fair trial. Putnam was too good a liar." His eyes focused on me for the first time. "Leave me alone. I've had a stomach full of the press." He limped off down the path toward Central Park West. He favored his left leg when he walked like he might need a knee replacement. Could he lift all those cement blocks to crush Tommy to death? The killer's letter implied he wasn't in the best physical shape. That would fit.

I hurried back to the *Gazette* to call Christine. She needed to know the lead I developed with Coogan. My hand hesitated over the phone. Should I risk putting her onto another dead end like

Julia Rains? I decided to let Christine make the decision. As Harry said, it's the cops' job to catch the crooks.

"Detective Carr."

"This is Butch, Christine. Can you talk for a minute?"

"Yeah. We're still tracking down Edwina Stone. I've been on the phone all morning trying to convince Putnam subcontractors to open up about disagreements with Tommy Putnam. Funny how much sway a billionaire holds, even after he's been squeezed to death. Nobody wants to talk."

"I may have a lead for you." I described the newspaper article in the morgue about Putnam and Coogan and my meeting with Coogan in the park. "He's bitter about Putnam lying at his trial, and guess who the judge was? Hawthorne."

"That sounds promising. I'll follow up on it. Thanks for the tip, sweetie."

Did she just call me sweetie?

Chapter Sixteen

THE AVENGER TOOK THE Christmas holidays off. There were no more dead bodies and no letters. Christine called me at the paper every so often with off-the-record updates on the cops' progress, or lack of it, with the Hawthorne and Putnam cases. They hadn't found Stone yet, but they were still looking. A few possible leads to improperly controlled propofol came in as a result of my reporting, but when Christine checked the hospitals, the problems were sloppy inventory practices and not real thefts. Harry told me murders not cracked within the first forty-eight hours usually go in the "unsolved" category. If that happened with the Hawthorne and Putnam cases, my crime reporting career could be stalled in its tracks.

David and Gene left for Greenwood, Mississippi after work on Friday before Christmas week. They invited me to go along, but I didn't feel right butting into a family gathering. They left me their apartment key and the Greenwood phone number if I needed anything, though what they would do from a thousand miles away wasn't clear. They were worried about The Avenger showing up at my apartment again, but none of us said it out loud.

The days before Christmas Eve were unseasonably warm. I read in the paper that some scientist at Caltech out in California claimed humans are ruining the atmosphere with our gasoline-powered cars and coal-burning furnaces. He said we're making everything warmer. If he spent some time in New York or Chicago in the winter, he might think that's not such a bad thing. Another researcher warned the world's population is increasing so fast that we'll soon run out of food. Wouldn't warmer weather give fruits and vegetables a longer growing season?

I pondered these weighty thoughts to avoid the task in front of me. I was sitting at my typewriter in the deserted newsroom on Christmas Eve. The light was off in Duke's office. Everyone had gone home after putting the next day's morning edition to bed. I was struggling to focus on next week's lonely hearts column. Dear Aunt Betty had stopped coming to work altogether two weeks before, so I assumed the duty in his place.

The insistent rhythmic tinkle of a Salvation Army Santa Claus's bell drifted up from the street corner below. In the dim, cavernous newsroom, my desk lamp cast a pale yellow glow against the white paper. I searched my mind for pithy advice to Puzzled in Poughkeepsie that didn't sound like "Get a life and quit being such an idiot."

I tapped the keys, "Dear Puzzled." The clicks of the keystrokes echoed loudly around the vacant desks. My thoughts drifted into a daydream about Christine in that blue sweater she wore when she came to my apartment to go through Judge Hawthorne's logs. I closed my eyes. The daydream became a vision of us sitting on my bed and me pulling the sweater over her head. Her long dark hair swished around her bare neck, and the little curl that creeps from the bun she wears when she's being a cop trailed across her cheekbone. I kissed the curl softly, and she moaned encouragement.

"Eleanor."

I jumped a mile and whirled around. "Walt! You scared me to death. I didn't know anybody was still here."

Walt lowered himself stiffly into his desk chair. "I was in the men's. Sorry I startled you." He looked around the empty room. "The place looks completely different without all the bodies, doesn't it? It seems we're the only ones with no place to go on Christmas Eve. Poor us." He opened his bottom desk drawer and pulled out a bottle of bourbon and two paper cups. "Join me?"

"Oh, no thanks, Walt. I'm about to pack up and head out. I appear to be suffering writer's block."

He poured two drinks anyway. "Nonsense, Eleanor. No self-respecting crime reporter ever turns down a free drink." He held a cup toward me. "As to your writer's block, authors in the romantic era believed some otherworldly power caused the blocks, some force that did not want them to write anymore. Wordsworth thought his dead sister's spirit caused his. Tell me what you're laboring over. Maybe I can help. Something to do with The Avenger?"

I took the cup. "No, just the next Dear Aunt Betty. Duke isn't expecting the finished product till Monday, but since I'm not rushing home to anyone, I figured I'd get it off my plate."

Walt held up his cup. "Cheers."

I drained mine. The alcohol burned all the way down, and I suppressed a cough. "Well, guess I'll get going."

He offered the bottle and raised his eyebrows. "Another?"

"No thanks."

He smiled with his mouth, but he had a funny, piercing look in his eyes. "What if I insist?"

We stared at each other for an awkward moment. My back stiffened. After years of knowing Walt, were things about to get weird? The only sounds were the Salvation Army bell and the swish of traffic below, then a sharp crack like a gunshot echoed across the room. The janitor stuck his head around the corner. "Sorry, I knocked over my broom. Didn't know you folks were still here."

I grabbed my coat and bag. "Night, Walt. Merry Christmas."

Dozing commuters and last-minute shoppers juggling brightly wrapped packages jammed the subway cars. I barely managed to squeeze in before the doors slid shut. Around the corner from my apartment, I stopped in the Middle Eastern take-out café for falafel and in the bodega next door for wine. I splurged on an expensive bottle, a Christmas gift to myself. Not exactly the roasted goose dinner from *A Christmas Carol*, but it would have to do.

I trudged up the stairs to my pitch-black deserted apartment, wishing I had thought to leave a light on when I ran out to work that morning. Once I got inside, I switched on every light and tuned the radio to an upbeat holiday music station. I was uncorking the wine when someone buzzed at the front door on the street. I went downstairs, fighting the irrational thought Walt Smith had followed me home from the paper. "Who is it?"

"It's Christine."

She was standing on the stoop holding a six-foot Christmas tree, a real one, and wearing the blue sweater. "I hope I'm not interrupting anything just showing up like this."

"Of course not." I nodded at the tree. "Where did you get that?"

"At the public market in Spanish Harlem, La Marqueta."

"How did you get here with it?" I pictured her in a cab with the tree sticking halfway out the side window.

"I walked. It's only a few blocks. I enjoyed lots of smiles and Merry Christmas wishes along the way." A chilly wind ruffled her hair.

"Come in. It's cold out here. Looks like the weather's turning." I took the top of the tree, and we carried it up the stairs to my apartment and stood it in the corner. "Beautiful."

She stepped back and surveyed the tree. "Nice, isn't it? I didn't bring any decorations." She held up a jar of caramel-colored liquid. "But I brought homemade eggnog."

"You made it?"

"Oh, no. It's specially concocted by Sister Francesca at La Marqueta."

"We can create our own decorations. I learned how to make snow at Merciful Heart. We just need soap flakes, cornstarch, and hot water."

Christine looked around my sparse kitchen. "You have cornstarch?"

I picked up the boys' apartment keys from the butcher block and jiggled them. "No, but I'll bet Gene does. And David no doubt has construction paper for decorations."

We found the cornstarch in Gene's pantry and red and green construction paper in David's desk. I made popcorn to string for a garland, and we cut out paper ornaments accompanied by carols from the radio. We propped a flashlight against a stack of books to spotlight the tree and stood back to appreciate our handiwork.

When I remember Christmas Eve 1971, I can close my eyes and recall all the sensations of that night. Blinking red lights from a neon sign across the street reflecting off the homemade snow on the tree, making it sparkle like glitter. Pine scent filling the room from the freshly cut evergreen tree. The thick eggnog tasting rich and syrupy with a spicy burn of brandy. "Silent Night" playing from my tinny little transistor radio. Christine's strong arms encircling me and pulling me in for a deep kiss.

Our first time wasn't the soft, gentle seduction of my daydreams. It was urgent fumbling with buttons, zippers, and buckles. We were like kids under the Christmas tree, tearing into the wrapping paper of a long-anticipated present. Afterward, we lay facing each other, letting our heartbeats and breathing get back to normal.

She kissed my lips. "You taste sweet."

My lips brushed the curl of dark hair on her cheek. "It's the eggnog and you down here." I stroked her, and she squirmed into the pressure of my fingers.

"Again?"

She moaned and pulled me on top of her.

Around two in the morning, it started to snow. When we finally slept, it was light enough to see the rays of sun reflecting off a blanket of white covering the streets and sidewalks. As I drifted off to sleep, she said, "I have a confession. Sister Francesca at La Marqueta is a witch doctor. She puts a love potion in her eggnog."

I nuzzled her cheek. "Interesting, but not necessary."

The next thing I knew, the click of my front door closing woke me. The sky had cleared after the snowstorm. I usually sleep like the dead and wake up a little disoriented. At first, I thought I must have dreamed the night before, but then the room with the Christmas tree came into focus. Last night was real, but Christine was gone. I threw on an XXL Ole Miss sweatshirt, David's castoff that came nearly to my knees, and ran to the window. She was already at the corner of 114th and Seventh Avenue. I watched her climb into a cab and disappear down the street.

I wanted to pound on the glass and yell, "What the hell?" but what good would that do? Then I noticed the piece of red construction paper on the butcher block with a note from Christine.

Butch, I'm a coward leaving you sleeping, but I need some time to think things through.

The old, long-ago insecure thought that I might have done something to disappoint her came rushing back. As a child, I wondered if my mother left me on Merciful Heart's doorstep because I fell short somehow. Back then, Sister Marie Madeline dried my tears and assured me I wasn't to blame. Where was a nun when you needed one?

You asked me the other night why I left Buffalo, and I gave you a lame answer about wanting a scenery change. The truth is, I ran away from a situation with a woman. I guess you'll think, just like I'm running away from you this morning. It's too hard to explain in a note. Please give me a few days. I'll call you. Christine

I crumpled the note and collapsed on the edge of the bed. Could I do as she asked and just wait for her to call me? Did I have any choice? I heard someone at the downstairs door. She came back! I threw open my apartment door to see David and Gene wrangling their suitcases into the foyer. "What are you doing here?"

"That's some greeting. Merry Christmas to you too."

"Sorry. I wasn't expecting to see you till tomorrow."

"Well, the family always opens presents on Christmas Eve, and everything after that is pretty much an anticlimax. Plus, we've been there for a week, and you don't want to overdo family. Plus, we heard there was a storm coming, and we didn't want to get stuck in Greenwood, so we took the red-eye out of Memphis last night."

Gene opened the door to their apartment. "Plus, we've been worried about you. Let us get settled and come down for a sandwich. We brought back a jar of David's grandma's pimento cheese, or as they call it in Mississippi, Dixie caviar."

David and I sat cross-legged around their coffee table, and Gene placed a heaping tray of sandwiches in front of us. "Fill us in on The Avenger murders."

"Indications are the same killer did both murders. The coroner found propofol in both victims' systems and the notes on the bodies and the letters he sent me about the two murders match. There's no other forensic evidence, as far as I know, no fingerprints. He's very careful, whoever he is. The police have one suspect so far, a convict who got paroled from prison two weeks before Judge Hawthorne was hanged, Edwina Stone. She's MIA, and they're still looking for her."

"The cops have no other suspects?"

"They're tracking down who might have bought propofol and whether Putnam, Junior made murderous enemies among his employees or subcontractors. As for the 'sins of the father' business in my letters and the notes left on the bodies, I seem to be alone thinking that's important. Sloane figures it's a distraction, like the Halloween cards and the Solar Cross symbol. Just this guy's play for attention in the newspaper. I've done some digging on my own about the sins of the fathers, and I've turned up two people who might have serious grievances against Professor Hawthorne and Thomas Putnam. Turns out, one appears to have an alibi. I've told the cops about the second one, but I'm afraid going after him would be a wild goose chase too. In his case, there may be a connection between Thomas Putnam, Tommy's father, and Judge Hawthorne."

"Who are the possible suspects you've turned up?"

"For the judge's murder, a woman named Julia Rains. The judge's father was a professor of early English literature at Columbia. Rains was a PhD candidate in the forties, a very big deal for a woman back then, and Hawthorne was her adviser. She spent months researching something about Chaucer's being the first guy to write in English. She told me all about it, but to tell the truth, I didn't quite follow. Anyway, the day before Julia was to appear before a committee to present her dissertation, she discovered her paper and all her research had been stolen. Professor Hawthorne was the only person who could vouch for her, but he mysteriously went missing. Turned out another of Hawthorne's students submitted Julia's work as his own and got the golden PhD ticket."

Gene took a big bite of his sandwich and moaned. "This pimento cheese is so good. But..." He held up his finger while he chewed and swallowed the bite. "But didn't she go to the police or to the powers that be at Columbia?"

"Yes and yes, but it all got swept under the rug. Rains says the thief's father made a two-million-dollar donation to the English department in Hawthorne's name. The professor died a few months later, and the whole thing got dropped."

"Sounds like she could be a promising suspect."

"I thought so too, but Rains claims she was at Parents' Night at the school where she teaches when the judge was killed, and I don't see any connection to the Putnams."

"What about the Tommy Putnam murder? You said you have a suspect related to the sins of his father?"

"Back in the late fifties, Thomas Putnam's testimony sent a politician to prison for bribery. I talked to the guy. He's a mess. He certainly holds a grudge against the family, but I'm not sure he'd be physically capable of pulling off two murders."

David gave me a sideways look. "You say you're alone in thinking there's more to the murders than revenge directly on the victims. What does Christine think? You haven't mentioned her name once. What's going on with you two?"

At that point, I lost it. I started blubbering so hard I couldn't get words out, and David grabbed me and held me till I calmed down enough to talk. "She came here last night with a real Christmas tree, and we had a wonderful evening, and she spent the night, but she ran out this morning before I woke up, and she left a note." I started blubbering again.

Gene pulled a handkerchief from his back pocket and handed it to me. "What did the note say?"

"She left Buffalo to get away from a woman, she called it a situation, and she needs time to think things through, and don't call her."

"What are you going to do?"

"What can I do? I either mope around like a whipped dog, or I call her and demand to know what her problem is."

"Darlin', there may be a middle ground."

"Like what?"

"You could go to her place and see if she's willing to tell you anything about what's bothering her. And if she is, you can listen like a friend."

"I can do that."

I ran upstairs, threw on some clothes, and took a cab to the Barbizon.

The lobby was buzzing with activity. A Christmas tree stood in the middle of the marble floor and rose to the top of the two-story atrium. Young women gathered in clumps with friends and family. Carols echoed off the walls.

I paced in front of the reception desk while the clerk telephoned Christine's room. She shook her head. "No answer."

What now? I turned to leave.

"Oh, miss? You might try the pool. In the basement. She sometimes swims in the morning."

Chlorine fumes filled a dimly lit basement hallway leading to the swimming pool. When I opened the double doors to the pool, heavy damp air hit me in the face. I waited for my eyes to adjust to the dark interior. A lone swimmer in a white bathing cap moved steadily along a swim lane in the Olympic-sized pool. Her strokes were so efficient she barely made a sound or raised a ripple. The water sheeted over her smooth shoulder and arm muscles. I watched her complete two more laps, and I almost lost my nerve. Christine was pretty clear when she asked me to give her a few days. As I backed into the door, she grabbed the edge of the pool, pulled off the swim cap, and shook out her dark hair.

"Christine."

She turned toward my voice. I felt a surge of relief when she smiled.

"Is it okay I came?"

"Given your personality, I suppose I'd have been more surprised if you hadn't come. I'm glad. I owe you an explanation." She levitated out of the water to sit on the edge of the pool. She was completely nude, giving me a full-frontal view of her breasts, slim waist, and flat stomach. I had to smile.

She looked down at herself. "As I said, no one ever comes down to the pool." She stood and shrugged into a white terrycloth robe, took my hand, and led me to a bench beside the pool. "Last night at your apartment, I wanted to be with you, and I planned it, but I wasn't being fair."

"I hope you know I want it too."

"Yes. But, Butch, I can't afford to get into another situation like the one I left behind in Buffalo."

David said listen like a friend. "What do you mean?"

"You asked me in the coffee shop why I left Buffalo, and I gave you a lame answer about wanting a scenery change. The truth is, I ran away because of a failed relationship with a woman." She tightened the sash of her robe. "You couldn't even call it a relationship. More an obsession on my part.

"Bella is a politician, on the Buffalo Common Council—that's like the City Council here. She has aspirations for higher office, mayor, or even governor, and I wouldn't be a bit surprised to see her attain them. She's married with two small children, and she's deeply in the closet. For the last year, my life has involved one lie after another. Sneaking around to steal time with her. Watching her in public appearances play-acting the perfect wife and mother. Hungrily hanging on her every word and gesture, looking for coded messages to me. Stalking her even. Disgusting."

She shivered. "As I look back on my last months in Buffalo, I was miserable, but with hindsight, I suspect she enjoyed the whole affair. She liked the intrigue. I was pathetic, terrified of making any demands on her that might drive her away."

"So what happened?"

"You won't be surprised it was about my work. When Bella and I met, I was a newly promoted commander in a challenging area of the city, high crime rate and not good community relations. I was the first woman to attain that rank. My area was in Bella's council district, which is how I met her in the first place. I built a great team, and we were making real progress, but things weren't moving fast enough to suit Bella. She wanted to run for mayor on a 'tough on crime' platform. She started putting pressure on me to manipulate crime statistics reporting so she could campaign on evidence of her effectiveness, showing she was reducing crime in her district while the rest of the city was seeing major increases. She asked me to downgrade felonies, throw crime reports in the trash, and discourage victims from filing complaints at all. I refused, of course."

"Of course. You would never do that."

"At first Bella begged and cajoled. She tried convincing me that once she got elected mayor, we could work together to implement all my reform ideas citywide. I'm ashamed to admit I was tempted for an instant. I was that crazy about her. But I just couldn't do it. When I wouldn't relent, she got nasty. She threatened to out me and pressure the chief to take away my squad."

"But if she outed you, she'd be outing herself."

"She wasn't being rational. She turned into someone I didn't recognize. She threatened to accuse me of stalking her and pushing myself on her."

"She's evil."

"The worst part was how badly she misjudged my character, to think I'd go along with the scheme. This morning at your apartment in the cold light of day, it hit me. I asked you to hold off reporting on the killer's second letter and about our suspect Edwina. How is that much different than what Bella wanted of me?"

"You had a reason. You felt my reporting the details might make catching the killer harder."

"Bella had her reasons too. Here's how the situation is different. I ran away, and you went ahead doing your job. I care about you, and I don't want to start a relationship risking a conflict because of this case."

"Is it about the case, or do you still have feelings for her?" I held my breath for the answer.

"I have feelings about her, but not in the way you're asking. I was obsessed with her for months, so I'm going to take some time to get over that. I'm still trying to sort out how I could have misjudged her so completely."

She tucked the curl behind her ear. "I went to your apartment hoping we would be together. I counted on the tree and the eggnog and signals I think I've been picking up from you."

"I don't have a good poker face. David guessed my feelings for you, and even the waitress in the Barbizon coffee shop has my number."

We sat next to each other in silence. My heart felt like it was shrinking in my chest. "Couldn't we just agree to keep our jobs and our relationship separate?"

"We can try. But for now, let's take things a step at a time. Let's get these murders behind us. If you're going to be a crime reporter and I'm going to stay an NYPD detective, we've got to figure out how to avoid professional conflicts. One thing I can promise, I'll never again ask you not to do your job."

"And I promise to consider everything off the record unless you tell me it's on."

"It's a deal." She stood up, opened the sash of her robe and let it drop to the pool deck, and pulled me to my feet. "Come in the water with me."

I looked across the Olympic-sized pool. Little ripples on the surface caused a play of light on the bottom, reflecting the flickering fluorescent tubes on the ceiling. "It looks deep." I backed up a step. "I've got a confession. I can't swim."

She took my face in her hands and kissed me and began unbuttoning my blouse. "It's shallower on this end. Don't worry. I'll hold you up."

I unhooked my pants, and she held my hands at my sides. "Let me."

I closed my eyes and forced myself to stand still. The world melted away. The vexing Avenger murders, my ambition to be a legitimate crime reporter, and my fear of sinking to the bottom of the swimming pool disappeared. Christine's fingers and her little nibbles on my skin filled up the space.

She stepped over the edge of the pool into the water and guided me in after her. The water was cool, but not unpleasant. "Just lie back on top of the water, like you're on a feather bed." She supported me with her hands behind my neck and in the small of my back. "If you can relax all your muscles, you'll float like a cork."

A scene from seventh grade popped into my head. Sister Rose, our general science teacher saying, "Fluids have surface tension, allowing bodies that are heavier than the liquid to float."

Betsy Culp, the most popular girl in our class, raised her hand. "Sister Rose. Have you ever been swimming?" I laughed along with everyone else, picturing Sister Rose's heavy body in a bikini and her stiff white-and-black wimple on her head. But late that night, in my single cot in the dark quiet of our dormitory room, I prayed to Baby Jesus to forgive me for making fun of Sister Rose. I knew what it felt like to be shamed about your body.

The memory made my legs start to sink, and I focused on relaxing the muscles. Sure enough, they floated back to the surface. "Hey, this works."

Christine guided me across the pool, like a tugboat pushing a mini barge. When we reached the far edge, in the deep end, I tensed up and my legs sank again. My breath caught when my feet couldn't find the bottom.

Christine held me steady against the tile and began kissing me and caressing the inside of my thighs with long, languid strokes.

"Are you sure no one ever comes down here? There were lots of people in the lobby."

"Yes, I'm sure, but if I'm making you uncomfortable, I'll stop." She said it like she knew what my answer would be.

"Don't stop." I was helpless, but in a good way, totally in her hands. Was this what she called taking our relationship a step at a time? Worked for me. I clung to her and buried my face in her shoulder while she made slow love to me, like in my fantasy. We could work everything else out. I just knew we could.

Chapter Seventeen

DUKE SAT IN HIS glass-enclosed office, hunched over his desk. He was hatless, so I figured he felt he had things under control. He peered through a magnifying glass at the morning edition dummy, preparing to sign off so the production department could start the presses.

I blew out a tired breath and gathered the pages of Aunt Betty's column for the next day's evening edition. I tapped them against the top of my desk to line them up and dropped them in my out basket for the copyboy to grab first thing in the morning. My phone shrilled, making me jump. Who in the world? "Hello. Tracy here."

"Good evening, Eleanor. You're working late."

The voice was muffled, as though the receiver was covered with a cloth or something, and the caller seemed to be purposefully lowering the pitch of his voice. I wouldn't be able to describe it or recognize it when the caller was speaking normally, but there was something familiar about the cadence. "It's good you're keeping your typewriting fingers nimble, because you're my scribe, and you're about to get another blockbuster story. Are you ready?" He chuckled.

I looked frantically around the deserted newsroom. Someone needed to hear what I was hearing. I stood and waved my arms madly to get Duke's attention. He remained deep in concentration over the dummy.

Keep the killer talking. "I'm glad to hear from you."

"Are you? Good." He giggled.

The sound sent a chill down my back.

"Well, let me fill you in on this evening's developments, then you'll want to rush over to Park and Seventy-Third to the office of Dr. William Griggs. He is a very successful plastic surgeon in our city. You may have met him in your travels around the fancy parties you cover for the paper. You'll certainly have seen his work in the faces and figures of his wealthy patients. He goes for the easy money: nose jobs, facelifts, and breast implants. He's not on the cutting edge of advances in surgical science." He stopped to snicker at his joke. The Avenger was in a great mood.

"Dr. Griggs has a very busy practice, and it's his habit to stay late in the evening on Thursdays, like tonight, catching up on his charting. I found him this evening alone and hard at work at his desk. He was quite shocked to see me standing in the doorway. I suppose the mask is off-putting. Understandable.

"His office reflects the success of his business. His desk is particularly interesting, seventeenth century and I suspect American-made in Boston. Particularly rare. I tried to put him at ease by admiring his collection of Peale miniatures. We could have enjoyed a discussion about them, but the good doctor was becoming more and more agitated, and I was afraid he would do something desperate, so I went ahead and injected him with the anesthetic."

Talk about agitated and desperate, I was desperate to get Duke's attention. "This is so interesting. Just let me get a pencil and my notebook. I don't want to miss any details." I threw a pencil at the glass wall of Duke's office. It worked. The ping against the window made him look up with a start. I pointed at the phone frantically and mouthed, *It's The Avenger.* He dropped the magnifying glass and rushed out of his office to my desk.

I positioned the receiver so Duke could hear. "Go ahead. I've got my notebook. Ready."

"As we speak, Dr. Griggs is resting comfortably with his head on his remarkable desk. They tell me propofol provides a very refreshing, dreamless sleep. I hope you won't think it bragging, but each of these events is more flawlessly executed than the one before. Good planning makes all the difference. And experience is helpful, of course.

"My current effort is working perfectly so far. As it turns out, the important components are close at hand in the doctor's office. There are three elements required for an effective fire: oxygen, fuel, and a spark."

Duke and I eyed each other. He was going to set the doctor's office on fire!

"Dr. Griggs does much of his surgery in his office. This works best for his patients' need for confidentiality. He keeps a good supply of oxygen handy for the procedures. Check. His records room is packed with paper patient files which provide the fuel. Check. The third is the spark, and I have a rather elegant solution for that. I'll keep it as a surprise for you."

Duke traced little circles in the air and mouthed, *Keep him talking.* He pantomimed holding a phone to his ear. *I'll call Sloane.* He ran back to his desk and scooped up his phone to call the detective.

Maybe I could get The Avenger to talk about his motive. "Did you say you're planning to start a fire? With the doctor inside? As background for our newspaper story, what is your purpose?"

"Come, Eleanor. You and I both know Dr. Griggs will be paying for sins of the past, just as Judge Hawthorne and Mr. Putnam. I must go now and complete the event. You'll hear from me soon."

"Wait." I grasped at a way to keep the killer on the phone. "You said Park and Seventy-Third? I'll hurry right there, but what should I look for when I arrive?"

"Oh, that will be clear. But you must hurry." The line went dead.

Duke slammed his phone down and ran back to my desk.

I replaced the receiver. "He hung up."

"Sloane's not there."

Duke and I stared at each other with our mouths open. He recovered first. "Do you know who this guy is?"

"No! I have no idea. It is a guy, though, right?"

"I think so, but I couldn't swear to it. He was masking his voice." He consulted his watch. "I can hold the presses half an hour but no longer."

"He said Park and Seventy-Third."

"Get over there right now and call the story back to me. I'll write it up. I'll keep trying to get hold of Sloane."

I dialed David. Thankfully he answered right away. "Meet me at Park and Seventy-Third with your cameras." I slammed the phone down, grabbed my coat off the back of my chair, and took the stairs two at a time. I caught a taxi just letting off a passenger at the curb in front of the *Gazette* building. At 65th, two fire trucks screamed around us, sirens blaring and lights flashing.

Police cruisers blocked the intersection of Park at 73rd. I paid the cabbie and ran around the corner. Four firetrucks and two ambulances lined the block in front of a brownstone totally engulfed in flames. The fire reflected off a brass plate to the right of the front door: WILLIAM J. GRIGGS, JR., MD.

David arrived just after I did with his equipment slung over his shoulders. He set up in front of the building and began popping flashbulbs. Firemen in helmets and bright yellow jackets with reflective tape on the chest and sleeves swarmed the scene like ants. Billowing black smoke poured from broken windows, and intense heat came in waves even as far as across the street where I stood. But what was most surprising was the noise. The roar from the fire inside the building sounded like some giant angry wild animal. It blanketed the shouts of firemen and sirens of firetrucks and ambulances rushing to join the fight.

The front door of the brownstone banged open and two firemen came down the steps carrying a body. When they got halfway to the sidewalk, the roar of the fire behind them intensified and the whole left side of the first floor lit up with bright yellow flames.

EMTs rushed to strap an oxygen mask on the victim and swung open the doors of the ambulance. They loaded him in the back and took off, siren blaring. The two rescuers dropped onto the curb and took off their helmets.

A fireman with CAPTAIN on his helmet bent over to talk with the two men on the curb. The younger one held up his hands, and the captain pointed toward an ambulance.

I approached the fireman on the curb. "Hey, let me get you some water or something." I ran to the ambulance and collared a tech and begged for a bottle of water from him.

The fireman chugged the whole thing. "Thanks."

"I'm a reporter from the *Gazette*. Can I talk to you for a minute?"

He swiped his forehead with his sleeve, leaving a black soot mark across his face. "I need to get back."

"Of course." I nodded toward the young fireman. An EMT was wrapping his hands in white gauze. "Is he going to be okay?"

"He'll be okay. It's his first call. He's my son."

"Quite an initiation for him."

"He's tough, and he's been well trained. He'll be fine."

"What did you see inside?"

"Travis, my son, ran in and I followed him. The victim was behind a desk, unconscious and tied to a chair. There was a file room off the main office. That's where the fire started. An oxygen tank in the corner had the valve full open. Travis ran to shut off the oxygen. That's how he burned his hands. I started to work on the ties around the victim's arms. We only had a few seconds to get out before a flashover."

"What's a flashover?"

"Technically, it's when every combustible surface exposed to thermal radiation in an enclosed space rapidly and simultaneously ignites."

That sounded like what they taught them in firemen's school. "What does that mean in laymen's terms?"

"All the paper records in that file room ignited in one giant flash."

"That's what happened as you came down the steps with the victim."

He nodded. "You won't survive a flashover. It instantly sucks all the oxygen from the space and heats the whole place to eleven hundred degrees. When you see the conditions for a flashover, you have seven seconds to get out. We barely escaped with the victim. One thing was weird. There was a gun duct-taped to the oxygen tank."

"Did you say a gun?"

"Yeah, like a really old one you see in paintings of the Puritans." He stood up. "Thanks for the water."

"Right. I hope Travis is okay."

He didn't acknowledge the last part. He was already joining other firemen holding a huge hose blasting water through a broken window on the first floor.

I ran to the corner of Park and found a phone booth to call Duke. I described the scene, the conflagration going on in the two-story building, the firemen scrambling to get a handle on the fire, and the flashover the father and son survived as they rescued a man, probably Dr. Griggs. Duke didn't know what a flashover was either, so I had to explain it. The boss took down all the information. "I'll add this to the description of The Avenger's phone call and run it downstairs to Production."

"David's here and he's got art."

"I won't be able to hold the copy long enough to get his photos, but tell him to hustle in first thing tomorrow morning, and we'll run them in the evening edition. And Butch..."

"Yeah, boss."

"Great job." He hung up.

I leaned against the wall in the stuffy phone booth and took a moment to savor the compliment. Maybe Duke was starting to see me as a crime reporter.

I ran back to the building. Firemen trained all the hoses on the first floor. Detectives Sloane and Carr had arrived, and Sloane had the fire chief cornered. Christine stood behind Sloane taking notes. I got close enough to listen. "When your men went inside, what did they see, Captain?"

"We only got to the first floor. One victim as far as we can tell."

"Dead or alive?"

"Don't know."

"Can you tell how the fire started? Was it deliberately set?"

"Two of my men found the guy tied to a chair, so I'd say arson's a pretty safe bet. We won't know for sure until we can get in and take a look around."

"The fire may be related to two murders, and this may be a third. How long before my forensics team can get inside?"

The chief surveyed the building. "We're making good progress. Give us another fifteen minutes."

I pulled Christine aside. "The Avenger called me in the newsroom just before the fire started and told me to get over here."

"You're kidding! Tell me about the call."

"I'm pretty sure it was a man. Duke thinks so too. He disguised his voice, but his speech pattern reminded me of the letters. He called me his scribe again. He said he was phoning from inside the doctor's office, and he had everything he needed to start a fire."

"Did he give you any clue about why?"

"He said the doctor is paying for sins of the past. Christine, he bragged he's getting better as he gains experience. He's planning more murders, I just know it."

"I have news too, about Edwina K. Stone. Bad news."

"What?"

Before Christine could finish, Sloane yelled in our direction. "Carr. The captain's given us the go-ahead to get inside."

David and I followed the detectives and two forensic techs into the building. Off the foyer to the left, in the burned-out office, water stood in puddles on the floor and dripped from the ceiling. The office furnishings were charred and ruined, including the seventeenth-century desk The Avenger described on the phone.

I tapped Christine on the shoulder. "The Avenger talked about that desk when he called. He went on about how rare and valuable it was, evidence of Griggs's success."

One tech began gathering and bagging odd bits of potential evidence that survived the fire and water, including short rope lengths knotted around the desk chair arms where The Avenger tied Griggs. Another tech went to work with a little brush to lift prints on the chair.

I whispered in Christine's ear. "Wouldn't the fire wipe out fingerprints?"

"That's a common misconception. Not always. We catch lots of arsonists because they assume they don't have to worry about prints and they get sloppy. The fire leaves behind fingerprint residue, but don't ask me how it works exactly."

A tech motioned for Christine's attention and pointed to the floor under the desk. A waterlogged piece of paper with red crayon print floated in a puddle.

I bent over and read it aloud. "I will repay. In due time their foot will slip; their day of disaster is near and their doom rushes upon them." It was signed with the Solar Cross with a red dot almost at twelve o'clock. I turned to ask David to get a shot, but he was way ahead of me. A flashbulb popped.

Christine spoke to the tech. "Can you pick it up without ruining it?"

The tech pulled two pieces of blotter paper from his tool kit, lifted the note with tweezers, and sandwiched the wet page between the blotters to dry.

David had moved on with his cameras to the patient file room. "Detectives, you'll want to see this." The chief and I followed Christine and Sloane into the ten-by-ten space. The flashover's intense heat had twisted the open metal shelving into weird curlicues and burned most of the paper files to ash.

The chief looked around the room. "This is where the fire started."

Sloane scratched his head with his pencil eraser. "And now I've seen everything." He pointed toward one corner of the compact space to an intact oxygen tank with an antique musket duct-taped around its middle.

I flipped back in my notebook. "Here's what he said on the phone."

Sloane looked up from his notes. "What do you mean, what he said on the phone?"

Christine stepped between us. "Someone called Butch just before the fire started."

"Well, what did he say?"

"He was ticking off the elements needed for a fire: oxygen, fuel, and a spark. About the spark, he said, 'I have an elegant solution for that.' Guess he meant the gun."

The chief squatted next to the oxygen tank. "I've seen these weapons in museums. It's an old flit-lock. When you pull the trigger, gunpowder causes a flash that would ignite any nearby fuel in the oxygen-rich environment. He piled paper around the tank. You can see the ashes." He motioned to Sloane. "Look at this. A remnant of a cord knotted around the gun's trigger. The rest of the cord must have burned away in the flashover. He could pull the trigger from a distance without the risk of being caught in the fire."

Sloane looked around the ruins of the patient files. "We won't get any information from his records on patients who might have an ax to grind with the doctor."

Christine spoke up. "This kind of medical work is usually cash on the barrelhead. Insurance doesn't pay for facelifts. We can find out who keeps his books. They'll have names and addresses on checks. I'll touch base with the state licensing people too. They'll have records of any malpractice complaints."

The latest murder note didn't mention the father, but it said, "I will repay." And it sounded like another Bible quote. Sloane was still intent that the motive was directly connected to the victim. Harry had been right about Sloane being a bloodhound on a trail and hard to convince otherwise.

Sloane sent a uniform out to a squad car to call about the status of the victim and to see if the station could identify a next of kin. "Maybe the doctor was alive when they carted him off in the ambulance. We could finally get a break on this case if the victim can talk. Our killer may have slipped up."

The uniform came hurrying back. "He's at Presbyterian, alive and conscious. The head nurse says he's heavily sedated because of the pain, and if we want to talk to him we'd better get right over there. You never know how long he'll hold on."

"Next of kin?"

The cop checked his notes. "Wife, Pamela Griggs. Twelve East Seventy-Fourth."

"Fancy neighborhood."

"Yeah."

Sloane took a quarter out of his pocket and looked at Christine. "I'll flip you for it. The loser visits the wife. Winner hustles over to the hospital."

Christine won the coin flip and headed out the door with me and David trailing behind.

David peeled off to get his photos processed for the next day's evening edition, and Christine and I shared a taxi to the massive hospital campus bordering the East River. We rode the elevator to the Burn Unit on the third floor. The ward was dimly lit and eerily quiet. The only sounds were the whooshing breaths of artificial respirators and hushed clipped communications among the nurses. Glass-fronted rooms ringed a central nursing station. After some convincing, Christine got permission from the chief nurse to question Griggs, and we followed her into his room.

Dr. Griggs looked like a mummy, his entire body wrapped in white gauze. A light blanket covered his middle for modesty. A heart monitor beeped steadily in the background. The patient was awake, and he turned his head in slow motion toward us. The nurse went to the bedside and deftly pulled the respirator hose from his mouth. She knew her business. I hoped she'd stick around because Griggs appeared to my untrained eye to be on his last leg. I didn't want to be responsible when he stopped breathing altogether.

Christine looked at the nurse for permission to start the questions. She nodded.

"Dr. Griggs, I'm Detective Carr, NYPD. Can I ask you a few questions about the fire at your office?"

He nodded.

"Good. Just nod or shake your head."

"I can talk." His voice came out a breathy, hoarse croak.

Christine leaned in. "Perfect. Did you see the person who tied you up and started the fire? Was it only one person?"

"Yes. Injected me."

"Could you tell if it was a man or a woman?"

Griggs shook his head. "Ski mask and disguised voice." He clutched Christine's hand. "My Peale miniatures."

The Avenger mentioned that on the phone. Peel? Like orange peel?

Christine bent closer. "Your Peale miniatures?"

"Yes. Charles Willson Peale. The artist. Miniatures. On the shelf behind my desk. Very valuable. He admired them."

Griggs wasn't making any sense. *The man might be dying, and he's worried about some miniatures, whatever that is.* It wouldn't help his state of mind to know the fire destroyed everything in the office.

Christine tried to get him on track again. "The person who injected you. Was there anything about his looks that might help us identify him?"

"Aging skin on the hands. Solar lentigines."

"Sorry?"

"Liver spots. And a fringe of gray hair around the bottom edge of the mask."

Leave it to a plastic surgeon to notice the condition of somebody's skin and hair.

"Was there anything else that would help us find him? Did you recognize his voice? Did he say anything that could offer a clue to his identity?"

Griggs gripped Christine's hand tighter and tried to sit up. "He knew about my Peales." He began a coughing fit.

The nurse stepped forward, moved us away from the bedside, and placed the respirator hose back in his mouth. "That's all. You're making his condition worse. You have to leave now."

We waited outside the room for the nurse. "When can we come back? He may have important information for catching a killer responsible for two murders before he started this fire."

"The crisis will come within the next seventy-eight hours. If we can keep him from getting an infection, and if his lungs aren't too badly damaged, he may survive for a while."

133

Christine handed her a card. "Will you call me when we can speak to him again?"

The nurse took the card but gave Christine a look like, *Don't count on it,* and hustled back into the patient's room.

Christine took my arm, and her hand on my elbow sent a tingle through my stomach. She led me to a small waiting area outside the unit. She sat heavily on one of the chrome and plastic sofas and pulled me down next to her. "I told you there's bad news about Edwina K. Stone. We found her."

"Where did you find her and why is that bad news?"

"In Bellevue Hospital. She's been in a coma since a few days after she got out of prison, a week before Judge Hawthorne's murder. That's why she disappeared. She caught the losing end of a bar fight. She flirted with the wrong woman's girlfriend at L's Bar in the Village. Paramedics brought her to the emergency room without any ID so the hospital's been treating her as a Jane Doe until she woke up and told them who she was. A nurse in the ICU got in touch with Probation, and they called us. Stone couldn't have done the judge or the billionaire. The timing's impossible. We're officially back to square one with suspects for Hawthorne and Putnam. Now we've got another attempted murder on our hands."

"The doc's description didn't narrow things down much. He didn't add anything we don't already know from the letters except all that stuff about some miniatures. Do you know what he was going on about?"

"Peale was an eighteenth-century painter. His specialty was tiny portraits of wealthy colonists painted on ivory."

"How do you know that?"

"The Museum of Fine Arts in Boston exhibits several of his pieces. My family used to visit there every year on my birthday."

There was a lot about this woman and her family I didn't know. "Why was Griggs so obsessed with telling you the perp recognized them?"

"He seems to think the fact the killer admired them is a clue to his identity. They are pretty obscure works. Your average crook wouldn't be likely to identify them. You said he mentioned the doctor's desk on the phone. It's from the same period as the artist. And there's the musket. The killer's referencing a time in the colonies before the Revolution."

"I didn't see any miniature paintings in the office. Maybe The Avenger stole them." I glanced at Christine sideways. "Since you're out of suspects for the murders, are you willing to hear more about Coogan, the potential person of interest I've uncovered?"

"I need to hurry back to the fire." She leaned in close, and her breath tickled my ear. "I'll be stuck at the scene late, but can I see you tonight? You can tell me more about your person of interest then."

Chapter Eighteen

IT WAS AFTER ELEVEN when I finally stumbled up the front steps of the brownstone. David and Gene's light was still on, so I knocked on their apartment door. Gene answered wearing his teddy bear slippers again.

I peeked around him. "Are you two still up?"

"Yes, David just got in from delivering his photos of the fire to the paper. We're having hot chocolate. Want some?"

"Yum. Sounds good. Christine's coming over when she finishes at the fire scene. Can she join us?"

David yelled from inside the apartment. "Of course she can."

Gene set mugs of steaming hot chocolate on the coffee table in front of each of us.

David grinned over the edge of his cup. "So you talked to Christine and you two worked it out. I knew you would. I know these things."

"You were right. I listened like a friend."

"I want to hear all about it, but first bring us up to speed on the doctor. Is he still alive? Could he tell you anything about who started the fire?"

"He's still alive, I think barely. He didn't recognize the fire starter. He couldn't say male or female for sure. He described someone with aging skin and gray hair."

Gene sat on the floor cross-legged. "I guess he would notice aging skin, being a plastic surgeon."

"That's what I thought too. The weird thing was he kept going on about his Peale miniatures, as though that might be some clue to the perp's identity."

"What's a peel miniature? Like an orange peel?"

"Not peel, P-E-A-L-E. He was a portrait artist or something."

"Just a minute." David got up, went to the bookshelf, and came back with a heavy textbook. "My art history from college. Let's see, Peale, Peale, Peale. Here he is, Charles Willson Peale, 1741-1827. He painted portraits of wealthy and famous people like Washington and Franklin, specializing in miniatures on ivory." He turned the book around so we could see examples of his works.

"How would that be a clue to The Avenger's identity?"

"Dr. Griggs might think it's pretty obscure information for a killer to know. It could narrow the field of suspects. It's from the same period as the musket he used to spark the fire. He's showing some connection to the Colonial Period."

Gene stroked his chin like Sherlock Holmes. "Hmm. This case may be even more complicated than you're thinking."

"What do you mean?"

"About those Bible verses the killer quoted in the notes and letters...the word 'father' in the Bible didn't always mean literally dad. It could mean forefathers."

David snapped his fingers. "Gene's right. Remember all those 'begets' in the Old Testament? So-and-so begat so-and-so. We used to have to read them aloud in Sunday School at Greenwood First Baptist. Whoever wrote the Bible was obsessed with genealogy."

"And now all these clues to the Colonial Period. You may have to trace the families back generations to find the connection."

"Wait a minute, Gene. You're telling me I may have to dig through all their ancestors to find a connection. How would I even do that?"

Gene rubbed his hands together. "No problem. The Public Library has a genealogy section. I'll help you. It'll be like a real-life game of Clue."

I grabbed Gene and gave him a big hug. "You're sweet, but first I'll check the clippings morgue one more time for Dr. Griggs's father. Who knows? He may tie the whole thing together."

Upstairs, my phone rang. "That may be Christine." I ran up the stairs and grabbed it on the third ring. "Hello."

"I saw you at the fire with your policewoman girlfriend."

The Avenger! His voice was masked again, and he followed up the remark about Christine with his creepy little giggle. *He has my home phone number.* He had been at the fire watching the whole time, and he could well be watching me now. I went to the window and parted the curtains a crack to look out. The buildings along Seventh Avenue cast shadows across the sidewalk, obscuring my view of the phone booth on the corner of 114th.

"Yes, it was just as you said it would be. Well planned and executed. Spectacular."

"Why, thank you, Eleanor. If you could see my face, I'm blushing. I have come a long way in my skills from when I first began the reckoning. Will I read your story in the morning edition?"

"Oh, yes, but David's photos will have to follow in the evening paper. By the way, what can I call you? It's awkward not knowing your name."

"All in good time. For now, you can continue calling me The Avenger. I rather like the nickname."

"I need answers to some questions to do your story justice. Can we meet in person?"

"Sadly, no. I can't risk that. But we're almost to the end. The next chapter will be our last. I'm afraid even the inept Detective Sloane will soon find a way to identify me. I just can't let that happen before the final tableau."

"What will the final tableau be?"

"Have you heard of the swimming test?"

I grabbed my notebook. "Did you say swimming test?"

"Yes. In the sixteen hundreds, the rabble crowd dragged accused witches to the nearest body of water. Some cleric, being the hypocrite he was, blessed the water. The crowd then stripped the accused to their undergarments, which as you can imagine would have been horribly degrading back in that time. They bound them and tossed them in the water to see if they sank or floated. The ignorant hordes believed that since witches spurned the holy sacrament of baptism, the blessed water would reject them and prevent them from submerging. An innocent person, not a witch, would sink like a stone, embraced by the holy water. A guilty one would float."

"But if innocent people sank to the bottom, wouldn't they drown anyway?"

"Victims had a rope tied around their middle so they could be pulled out if they sank, but, of course, there were numerous accidental drownings. People justified their actions by telling each other they were letting a higher power decide the outcome."

A siren whizzed past. I heard the sound on the phone an instant before a police car sped down the street outside my apartment. *He's calling from the corner phone booth.* The front doorbell buzzed. Christine!

"I see you have company. I await your article about Dr. Griggs with bated breath. Stay tuned for the final episode of our series. Goodbye, Eleanor." He hung up.

I rushed down the stairs and threw open the front door. Across the street, the phone booth was empty with the folding door standing open. Christine followed my gaze. "What is it?"

"The Avenger. He just called me from that booth on the corner."

She touched her gun inside her suitcoat, ran to the booth, and looked up and down the street. She shook her head and walked back. Her usually crisp white shirt was rumpled, showing the signs of her long night at the fire scene. I hugged her.

She held me close, reluctant to let go. "I probably smell like smoke."

"Never mind. We both do. Christine, I have a gun. Should I start carrying it?"

"A gun? Where did you get a gun?"

"It's David's. His grandpa gave it to him. It's not loaded."

"Do you know how to use a gun?"

"No. I thought I might scare someone with it."

"You never want to point a gun at someone if you're not prepared to use it. Show me."

I led her into my apartment and took the leather case down from its hiding place on top of the kitchen cabinet. She unzipped the case and shook six bullets out of the side pocket. "When we have time, I'll take you to the police range and show you how to shoot it. In the meantime, I'm going to load it but put it back on top of the cabinet. Don't take it down unless you absolutely have to."

I watched her load the bullets into the cylinder. "For now, I'll show you the bare minimum. This is the safety. You flip it up like this, aim, and squeeze the trigger. Don't pull, squeeze."

"You think I might have to use it?"

"No. He sees you as his partner right now, but he's unpredictable. Just forget you have it until we can get to the range." She zipped the loaded gun in its case and stowed it back on top of the cabinet.

"David and Gene and I were having some hot chocolate."

"That sounds so good."

Gene let us in and rushed to fill another mug for Christine. David scooted over to make room on the couch for her.

I told Christine and the boys details of the phone call from The Avenger. "He was in the phone booth across the street. If you had looked out your window, you would have seen him. He said there will be one last murder. He called it 'the final episode.'" I looked at my notes. "He talked about a 'swimming test' they used to do on accused witches in olden days. They threw a person in the water with their hands and feet tied. If they sank, they were innocent, and if they floated, they were a witch."

Gene made his Sherlock Holmes move again, stroking his chin. "Huh? That sounds backward. Wouldn't the innocent people drown?"

"I guess the mob didn't think that through very well. Anyway, if we don't find The Avenger soon, he'll carry out the last murder and we may never catch him."

Christine blew a tired breath that fluttered the wisps of dark hair around her face. "We got a call from Presbyterian. Dr. Griggs didn't make it. Now we have three murders on our hands, and we're no closer to the killer than we were after the first one. The police commissioner showed up at the fire scene just before I left. He ordered Sloane to come to his office first thing tomorrow morning to brief him on our progress, and Sloane wants me to go with him. I guess Tina Putnam has complained to the mayor, and he's on the commissioner's back about unsolved murders of prominent citizens."

Christine drained her cup, and Gene jumped up to get her a refill. "No, thanks. I have to get home for a shower and then meet Sloane at the precinct to prepare for the commissioner meeting. The forensics techs picked up some partial prints at the fire scene. If we're lucky, we'll have some progress to show." She rubbed her eyes. "No sleep tonight."

I walked her to the corner. "Can't you stay here with me and grab a few hours' rest?"

"Can't afford to. You said yourself, we have to find this guy, now or never. He may have screwed up leaving prints at the Griggs fire. I'll call you tomorrow after we meet with the commissioner."

"I'll be at the clippings morgue as soon as Scotty opens up. Maybe Griggs holds a key to the connections among the victims."

Chapter Nineteen

I HEARD SCOTTY WHISTLING down the hall as he stepped off the elevator the next morning. "Eleanor, good morning. You're here bright and early." He took the morning edition of the *Gazette* from under his arm. "I scanned your story on Dr. Griggs over coffee. Good work."

"Thanks, Scotty. But the bad news is the doctor didn't survive. I'm here to look up his father. The brass plaque on the front of his office said he was a junior, so we're looking for William, Senior. I hope there will be a clue this time that ties all the victims together."

Scotty fished around in his pocket for the key to the morgue. "Let's take a look." He took off his suitcoat and hung it over the back of his desk chair and rolled up the sleeves of his starched dress shirt.

He climbed the ladder to the card catalog drawer for G and pulled a card. "Here's William Griggs. No indication of junior or senior, but let's track down the file and see what we've got."

I followed him along a row of steel filing cabinets. He opened one and pulled a slim file. "Here you are."

The file held several pages, a supplement story dated 1955 from *This Week*, the photo magazine the *Gazette* puts out every Sunday. The article was titled "Execution of an Innocent: The Sad Story of Reverend George Burroughs." The byline was Walter Smith. This must have been one of the first stories Walt wrote for the *Gazette*.

"Sit over here, Eleanor." Scotty pushed his papers aside to make a place for me at his desk. Underneath the title, a color illustration showed a man in chains kneeling before a gallows. A cluster of formally dressed official-looking men stood next to him, whispering behind their hands. I settled in with my notebook to read the article.

The wooden oxcart bounced and swayed along the rutted dirt path from the Salem Village meeting house toward Proctor's Ledge. Reverend George Burroughs stood with his short, muscular legs spread far apart and braced his back against the rough plank side of the cart. He was unwilling to kneel with the other prisoners, three men and one woman, on the cart floor among the remains of straw and chicken feces. Heavy chains hanging from manacles on his wrists swayed in time with the oxen's plodding steps and caused the rough iron bracelets to bite into his skin.

Marching two by two in front of the team of oxen, Salem Village leaders and court magistrates in black wool frockcoats, despite the sweltering August sun, set a solemn slow pace. They appeared in no rush to arrive at the gallows.

The procession bumped past the Congregational Church where Burroughs had ministered to parishioners for a short and turbulent time ending the year before. Someone was ringing the steeple bell, tolling the passing of the macabre parade. At the edge of the village, the path curved around a granite outcropping, and the throng of villagers who were gathered on Proctor's Ledge to witness the hangings came into view. Burroughs recognized most of them. Some stared in the direction of the cart but avoided his eyes. Some focused on the ground. His accusers, in the front row closest to the gallows, glared directly at him.

High Sheriff George Corwin looked over the proceedings with his arms folded. He had chosen the Ledge as the hanging site and had signed the arrest warrant that forced Burroughs back to Salem Village to stand trial as a witch. The crowd parted to let the oxcart pass. It groaned to a stop beside the gallows where five nooses swung gently in the hot breeze.

Corwin pulled Burroughs roughly from the cart. The other condemned prisoners struggled to their feet. The woman, Martha Carrier, hesitated on the edge. Burroughs took her arm to help her down. She jerked away from his grasp. "Mind your own self,

George Burroughs." A low murmur rippled through the crowd. Martha's defiant spirit was one of the reasons she found herself facing death by hanging. At her trial, when the judges offered her the opportunity to admit being a witch and save her life, she stubbornly refused to confess to "a falsehood so filthy."

Sheriff Corwin pushed the prisoners into a ragged line and nodded toward the magistrates. Judge John Hathorne stepped forward and cleared his throat. "Upon the authority vested in this court by William and Mary, by the Grace of God, of England, Scotland, France, and Ireland, King and Queen and defenders of the faith, you stand convicted of sundry acts of witchcraft, inflicting great hurt and bodily damage, confederacy with the Devil, as well as other detestable acts. You are hereby sentenced to be hanged by the neck until you are dead. May God have mercy on your souls."

For a moment no one seemed to know what came next. A crow's croak from a pine tree at the edge of the clearing broke the spell. Someone in the crowd yelled, "Last words."

Burroughs stepped out of line and gazed defiantly around the crowd. "Citizens of Salem Village. You called me to this community to minister to the Lord's flock. Not one of you dare say that I ever failed to diligently guide you in your spiritual journey, comfort you in times of sorrow and loss, and teach God's holy word. But you have fallen into the Devil's snare. Your community has turned against itself. Quarrels about money, land, competition, and feuds have turned into accusations and executions."

He pointed with a manacled hand. "Dr. William Griggs. You ignited this hysteria by diagnosing the behavior of naïve, attention-hungry girls as evidence of their suffering under an Evil Hand. You claim to be a man of science. I call on you to deny these superstitious fantasies and admit you were motivated by a wish to eliminate competition from the midwife, Elizabeth Proctor. This virtuous woman was convicted of being a witch. She was spared the noose because she was with child, but in the eyes of the law she is a dead person, separated from society."

He called out three other men in the crowd. "James Greenslit, Samuel Webber, and Simon Willard. You testified under oath to having witnessed me perform feats of superhuman strength that could only have been done by a sorcerer. You told the judges you saw me hold a heavy musket with only a finger and lift full molasses and cider barrels with one hand. I admit to being strong, but my robust nature comes by the Grace of God, not the dark force of Satan.

"I do not blame you. You are under the influence of the real villain in this sad story." He turned to a couple in the front row. "Thomas Putnam and his wife, Ann Carr Putnam. You accuse me of straying from the path of Puritanism. Despite your great wealth and abundance of property, you feel control and power the Putnam family has exercised for many years over this community slipping from your grip. You have used grievances over old, settled debts against me to punish me.

"Magistrate Hathorne, you entreat God to have mercy on my soul. I rest easy in God's mercy. I say may God have mercy on all your souls."

Burroughs fell to his knees and raised his hands toward the sky. "Our Father who art in heaven…"

A collective gasp rose from the crowd. A witch was incapable of reciting The Lord's Prayer.

"Hallowed be thy name." In his sonorous preacher's voice, without wavering or hesitating, Reverend Burroughs recited the prayer through. "For thine is the kingdom, and the power, and the glory forever. Amen." A cloud passed over the sun, and the hot breeze turned suddenly chilly.

A voice from the crowd yelled, "The man is innocent. He said the prayer. Let him go. Let them all go." Others in the throng joined in, taking one side or the other. "Don't be fooled. The Devil gave him the words." "What about his two dead wives? Their spirits came to me in the night. They said he killed them." "He's a man of God. How can we judge him?"

A voice from the back of the crowd rose over the rest. "Good citizens of Salem Village, be still and listen." A man, dressed in the formal gear of a minister, sat astride a white horse.

Whispers circulated through the crowd. "It's Reverend Cotton Mather traveled here from Boston."

The minister passed his hands over the crowd as though to both bless and quiet them. "This man of God, as you call him, is not ordained in His holy eyes. He does not take the sacrament of the Lord's Supper, and he refuses to baptize his children. He has been tried and found guilty in their Majesty's court by these good magistrates. The Devil is testing us. We must remain resolute."

Sheriff Corwin pulled Burroughs to his feet and shoved him up the stairs of the gallows. He looped the noose over Burroughs's head.

All motion and sound stopped, and even the breeze died. Burroughs bowed his head. "Make the knot tight, Sheriff."

Without a word, Corwin pulled the lever to release the trap door beneath Burroughs, and the minister's body dropped with a sickening thud. His feet jerked twice, then hung dead still.

Reverend George Burroughs, along with the other four prisoners hanged that day, was buried in a shallow grave among the rocks of Proctor's Ledge. He was the only minister to be executed during the time known as the Salem witch trials.

"Wow!"

Scotty jumped. "What did you find?"

"They're all here—Putnam, Griggs, and Hathorne. The magistrate's name is spelled differently. Do you think that could be a typo?"

"Let me see." Scotty took the article. "Remember, the judge's obit mentioned he was the great-grandson of Nathaniel Hawthorne. I read somewhere the novelist changed the spelling of the family name because he was embarrassed about his ancestor's role in the witch trials. That would fit."

"The Avenger murders must be retaliation for the executions of accused witches in the sixteen hundreds. This story ties together not only the names of the victims, but also The Avenger's references to witches and the Colonial Period."

Scotty nodded. "And the methods of the murders. Hanging, burning, and being pressed to death were all favored retribution for accused witches."

"The Avenger told me he's planning one final murder. He must be targeting a descendant of the other principals, High Sheriff Corwin, or the other accusers. I need to Xerox this article, Scotty, and get it to Detective Carr right away."

Scotty showed me how to use the Xerox machine the size of a Volkswagen. I copied the article and ran upstairs. Walt wrote the piece about Burrough's execution back in 1955. Maybe he could shed more light on it. Walt's desk behind mine was empty, not just like he was away but looking abandoned with the typewriter covered and his chair pushed under the desk. Jake, the sports guy, ambled by. "Jake, have you seen Walt?"

"He called off sick." He stopped and looked around the room. "Don't say I told you, but I hear it's serious. He's on extended sick leave."

My phone rang. Jake hovered, anxious to hear any good gossip about The Avenger. Seemed to me he had way too much time on his hands. I answered the phone, and Christine said, "It's me."

"Just a minute." I put my hand over the phone. "Got to take this, Jake. Thanks."

"Sure." He wandered off with his hands in his pockets.

"Sorry, Christine. A curious colleague. How did your meeting go with the police commissioner?"

"Off the record, right?"

"Right."

"He's far from happy. He ripped Sloane a new one. Threatened to turn the whole thing over to the Feds if we don't have some significant progress he can report to the mayor. He gave us a week."

"Did the fingerprints from Dr. Griggs's office pan out?"

"We got some partials. Ironically, Sloane got the jump on the commissioner. He has already reached out to the Feds. We sent the prints off to Quantico to the FBI lab for analysis. Hopefully, we'll get something back today. Did you find anything in the clippings morgue?"

"I think I found something really important. Maybe the link that ties the three murders together. Can I come over to the precinct and show you?"

"I'm home. I'm going to swim a few laps then try to grab a couple hours of sleep while we wait for fingerprint results." She yawned in my ear. "Sorry. Can you bring it to the hotel around three this afternoon?"

"I'll be there." I drummed my fingers on the desk. What could I do in the meantime? Figure out who The Avenger's next victim will be. I spread out the pages of Walt's *This Week* article and took out my notebook. I drew a line down the middle of the blank page and headed each column *Witch Trial* and *Avenger Murders*. I wrote *John Hathorne - Magistrate* and across from it *John Hawthorne – Judge*. The next line, *Thomas Putnam – Wealthy Property Owner,* and across under the second column *Tommy Putnam – Wealthy Property Owner.* Next, *William Griggs – Doctor and William Griggs – Doctor. High Sheriff George Corwin has to be the next one in line. I've got to find a cop named George Corwin and warn him.* I grabbed the Manhattan white pages from a shelf behind Duke's desk. There were four pages of Corwins, forty or so named George or with the initial G. Might as well get started. Before I could pick up my phone, it rang.

"Butch, it's Gene." He sounded short of breath like he'd just run a race. "Can you come to the apartment right now? I just got back from the genealogy section of the library. There's something I have to show you."

"What is it?"

"Just come in a hurry. It's too complicated to explain on the phone."

I grabbed the *This Week* article, ran down the stairs, and caught the subway, the fastest way home in the middle of the day. I was at the boys' door in fifteen minutes. Gene sat in the middle of the floor surrounded by books and papers and hand-drawn charts.

"What's up, Sherlock?"

"Sit down, sit down. I traced Hawthorne, Putnam, and Griggs's ancestors all the way back nine or ten generations to the early sixteen hundreds. Their families were not Johnny-come-lately to America. They go back to the original colonists. There was one glitch. The spelling of Judge Hawthorne's name changed along the way."

"Yeah, his great-grandfather changed it."

"How do you know that?" He was too excited to wait for my answer. "Anyway, the families converge in Salem Village, Massachusetts, and, get this, they were all principals in the Salem witch trials. John Hathorne was one of the magistrates who presided over the trials. Dr. George Griggs diagnosed the girls who were having fits in the first place."

I spread the *This Week* article in front of him. "And Thomas Putnam and his wife Ann Putnam, kept the hysteria going and filed all sorts of complaints against innocent people with the courts."

"That's what I wanted to tell you. Thomas Putnam and his wife, Ann *Carr* Putnam. Can you believe Detective Christine Carr is related to one of the primary accusers in the Salem witch trials?"

I grabbed the page from the article. There it was. Reverend Burroughs called out "Thomas Putnam and his wife Ann Carr Putnam." I had totally missed her maiden name. The brain itch came back. The one saying something's going on I need to pay attention to. The Avenger hinted the last chapter would be the swimming test. A motion picture of the pool in the Barbizon basement fluttered onto my mental screen. The wavering reflection of the fluorescent lights on the surface. Christine's terrycloth robe dropping in a heap on the pool deck. A dark figure in a ski mask lurking in the shadows.

"Can I use your phone?" I dialed the Barbizon. The front desk let Christine's phone ring ten times with no answer.

"I gotta go, Gene. Call Detective Sloane at the Ninth Precinct. Tell him to hurry to the Barbizon Hotel. The basement pool. Christine may be in trouble." I was halfway out to the street when I remembered the gun. I sprinted up the stairs two at a time to my apartment, grabbed the case off the top of the cabinet, and ran to the corner to hail a cab.

Chapter Twenty

ON THE WAY TO the Barbizon, I talked myself into and out of a state of panic. Christine left my apartment dead tired. She's probably just so sound asleep she didn't hear her phone. But she always answers on the first ring. But she's trained to deal with these kinds of situations. A killer who is not in the best physical condition couldn't overwhelm her, could he? I jumped out of the cab before it fully stopped rolling, almost forgetting the gun on the seat. I raced across the lobby to the front desk. "Christine Carr." She'd pick up this time.

The clerk let it ring. No answer.

I ran to the door leading to the basement and stumbled down the steps to the dim hallway. I stuck the gun, still in its case, into my waistband behind my back and listened at the door to the pool. I heard someone whistling through his teeth: "Yankee Doodle." I tried peeking through the small squares of glass at the top of the heavy double doors, but I was too short to reach. I took a deep breath and threw my weight against the doors. The scene inside was like in my mental movie, the fluorescent lights reflected off the water's surface and Christine's white terry cloth robe where she left it by the pool.

"Eleanor!"

By the back wall, a masked figure dressed all in black was testing the knots on nylon cord tied around Christine's hands and feet. She was nude and slumped in a metal folding chair with her eyes closed and her head lolled to the side.

"What a nice surprise. You're just in time to witness the final scene in person." He stripped off the ski mask.

It was Walt Smith. I can't say I was surprised. Somewhere in my brain, the itch felt scratched. What did surprise me was how sick he looked. His face was gray, and the skin on his jowls and neck hung slack. I glanced at the doors, willing Sloane or someone to come and save us. Why hadn't I told the desk clerk to bring the police? I touched the gun case in my waistband. What if Gene wasn't able to find Sloane? No one would come. Christine said she always had the pool to herself. Whatever happened would be up to me. Keep him talking. "This is the swimming test like you told me on the phone."

"Exactly right." Walt jerked on the cord around Christine's wrists to satisfy himself it was tight. "You'd better stand back a little, Eleanor. I trust I'm not going to have a problem with you resisting the preordained conclusion. I know she's your paramour, but you can understand how perfectly this is unfolding. When Detective Carr appeared on the scene, Christine Ann Carr, I immediately knew He had delivered the completion of my story, and your dalliance with her made things move along quite well."

Did he mean He, God, or He, the Devil had delivered Christine to him?

"He has been guiding my hand since the first."

"You mean since your first murder. Since you hanged Judge Hawthorne."

"Oh, the judge wasn't the first. Officer George Corwin was the first."

I sidled closer and sat on the edge of the bench. "Tell me about Officer George Corwin. I don't have my notebook, but I'll remember every word."

"It was in 1955. I was researching a story for *This Week* about the Reverend Burroughs lynching in Salem Village during the witch trials."

"I found your article in the morgue. Riveting."

"Why, thank you, Eleanor. The magazine editor gave me the less-than-desirable assignment because I was a rookie reporter, but the more I looked into the Burroughs story, the more I became convinced I was being called to assess justice for him. The ignorance and selfishness of the people of Salem Village was a stain on humanity that I needed to erase. I became enraged at his accusers and executioners."

Christine moaned softly.

"Shouldn't you let her lie down? She looks uncomfortable."

"Don't worry. I'm told the unconscious state brought on by propofol is quite pleasant." Walt bent over Christine to straighten her body on the folding chair.

While his attention was on her, I reached behind my back and unzipped the top of the gun case.

"I became obsessed. I couldn't eat or sleep or write. The paper was close to firing me. Finally, in desperation, I rented a car and drove to Massachusetts to see the setting of the case firsthand, hoping that might put things in perspective. I toured the Putnam home where Burroughs and his family lived his first months in Salem, the Congregational Church, and Proctor's Ledge where he proved his innocence by reciting the Lord's Prayer. They hanged him there anyway."

Walt began pacing. "Far from putting my mind at ease, being close to where Reverend Burroughs met his end heightened my disgust and anger. That's when He began communicating with me."

"About Officer Corwin?"

"In due time. I couldn't afford a hotel room in Salem, so instead of sleeping in the car, I decided to drive back to New York that night. You know how you are when you're young. Indestructible. Outside Port Chester, I suppose I was crossing the center line a bit, and a police car pulled me over on the dark deserted highway. The officer approached my car and shone a flashlight in my eyes. 'How much have you had to drink, sir?'

"Then I saw his name pin on his shirt, *Officer George Corwin*. It was a clear sign from Him. I said, 'I haven't been drinking, Officer Corwin. I'm just tired.'

"'I'll have to take you in just the same. Department regulations,' he said.

"The officer walked around the back of my car to write down the license plate. At that moment, He threw my car into reverse and pressed my foot down on the accelerator."

He'd said He again. "When you say He, do you mean God?"

Walt smiled. "Something bigger than what you call God. This is not the place to debate the power that leads me. Our time is short. We don't want Detective Carr to wake up, do we? Back to Officer Corwin. The bumper pinned the officer between our two cars. His scream was horrible. I expected people to come running, but no one did. Everything I needed was at hand. Officer Corwin had a shovel and a tarpaulin in the trunk of the patrol car. I buried him in the woods next to the road and drove back to New York. I washed the rental car thoroughly the next day and returned it without incident. I checked the Port Chester newspapers for weeks. They found his body, of course. The patrol car marked the spot where it happened. But they never connected the crime to me. I began sleeping soundly right away, and my appetite returned. I wrote the article you saw in an hour."

"Then why did you pick back up with Judge Hawthorne so many years later?"

"No time to go into it now. We don't want Detective Carr to wake up and experience any discomfort, do we?" He ran his fingers through her hair.

My stomach turned over. *Get your hands off her, you creep.*

He took a folded piece of paper from his pocket and read. "*An eye for an eye; a tooth for a tooth.* I'll just place this out of the way of any splashes." He bent over and propped the note against the wall. "Now, let us proceed."

Keep him talking. "I've heard that expression before. Where does it come from?"

"Deuteronomy. Moses addressing the Israelites on the Plains of Moab in 1400 BC. After forty years of wilderness wandering, they were about to enter the Promised Land. Their leader was enumerating God's laws they must faithfully follow in order to possess the land." He grunted and half lifted, half dragged Christine's limp body toward the edge of the pool.

Now or never. I scrambled up from the bench and pulled the gun from its case and held it behind my back. Flip up the safety, aim, and squeeze, don't pull, the trigger. "Wait. Don't you have to get a preacher to bless the water so it's a real test?"

"We'll have to approximate." He made the sign of the cross over the water.

He held Christine under her arms and struggled to shove her legs in the water up to her knees.

I aimed the muzzle of the gun at his belt buckle. "Stop."

He dropped her limp torso like a ragdoll and her head made a hollow cracking sound against the cement.

He stood up straight with his hands in front of him for an instant, then moved faster than he should have been able to toward Christine. I squeezed the trigger. The gun bucked in my grip, and a loud bang echoed around the tile walls. He kept moving toward Christine and shoved and kicked her into the water. She bobbed on the surface once, then sank straight to the bottom.

I dropped the gun and jumped in. Thank goodness the shock of the water revived Christine. Her eyes popped open. I grabbed her around the waist and walked along the bottom till I managed to push her head above water at the edge of the pool. I grabbed a breath and started working on the knots at her wrists. I got the ropes off and pushed her out of the water and struggled out myself. Christine sat up, looking dazed from the propofol and the blow to her head.

That's when I saw the blood. Walt lay on his side in a pool of it. The shot I fired hit him. I knelt next to him and felt his pulse. The doors burst open. Sloane, Gene and David, and a bunch of uniforms erupted into the room with a crowd of women behind them.

"Somebody call an ambulance!"

Chapter Twenty-One

CHRISTINE LAY STRETCHED OUT full length on my leather couch with her head in my lap. She raised up a little to take a sip of wine, and gingerly fingered the bandage on the back of her head. When Walt Smith dropped her on the pool deck, she got a huge lump and a concussion.

"Are you sure you should be drinking on top of the pain pills? And I wish you'd reconsider your decision to go back to work. Detective Sloane could have gotten by without you for another few days."

"Ease up, Nurse Nancy. I wanted to be in on the search of Smith's apartment this morning, and Sloane's going to interview him in Bellevue tomorrow. I can't miss out on that."

"Walt's going to recover, right?"

"He'll survive the gunshot wound fine. You shot him through the torso in just the right place to incapacitate him without killing him or hitting any major organs. Not sure how you managed it."

"I did just what you told me, aim and squeeze, don't pull, the trigger."

"The gunshot won't kill him, but the Stage Five prostate cancer will. He must have had symptoms for a while, but we can't find any indication he's sought medical treatment for it."

"That's why he was running to the men's room every ten minutes. Is the cancer the reason he started up the killings after so many years?"

"Could be. Maybe we'll find out when we question him tomorrow. The doctors at Bellevue say he'll never live long enough to stand trial."

"What did you find in his apartment?"

"The propofol. He had enough for several more injections."

"Where did he get the stuff?"

"Don't know yet. I never found any hospital that was missing the drug from their inventory. We found a used syringe beside an orange on his kitchen table. He had been practicing giving the injections. He was pretty proficient. I didn't even know what was happening when he stuck me in the neck."

I shivered at the memory of Christine's nude body, tied hand and foot, unconscious in the folding chair by the pool.

"We found shelves full of books about the Salem witch trials and genealogy references. On his desk, there were logs of the movement patterns of his victims. One whole wall was covered with photos, Judge Hawthorne heading into and out of the courthouse and even shots outside his home in Connecticut. Smith had pictures of Tommy and Tina Putnam in Central Park with their two boys and Tommy at the construction site, and of Dr. Griggs entering and leaving his office."

"And pictures of you?"

"Yeah. Shots of you and me that night we walked in the rain near the Barbizon and me standing outside your apartment holding the Christmas tree and several photos of us at the fire."

"We never noticed him."

"I was fixated on Edwina Stone. That's a lesson I need to learn from you. Keep an open mind and pay attention to gut feelings. That's what makes you a good crime reporter."

That was the best affirmation she could have given me. It felt like when Sister Marie Madeline reassured me about my mother and the girls' teasing. I kissed Christine on the forehead. "Thank you. Let's hope Duke agrees." I glanced at her. "I know what would convince Duke to let me do more crime reporting. If Sloane allowed me in Walt's hospital room when you interview him tomorrow."

"I might be able to get you in the room." She pulled me in for a long, deep kiss. "What do I get in return?"

Chapter Twenty-Two

THE FRONT ENTRANCE OF Bellevue looks like a red brick Sphinx. The north and south wings jut out like the paws, and the middle section rises like the giant head. An antique black wrought iron gate proudly announces BELLEVUE HOSPITAL. It's the oldest public hospital in the United States. The complex of buildings is like a small city with its own jail on the nineteenth floor.

Turned out Christine didn't have to convince Sloane to let me come to the interview. Walt insisted I be there. He told the detectives he needed his scribe present to hear the whole story. That and the fact I saved Christine from drowning did the trick.

We took the elevator up to the jail ward. It stopped on almost every floor to let doctors and nurses in blue scrubs bustle on and off. There were no casual greetings. Everyone had an important place to be, and they didn't waste time getting there. On the jail ward, two uniforms stood guard in front of Walt's door at the end of the hall. Sloane flashed his ID, and one officer opened the door.

Walt was propped up in bed, working on his *Times* crossword puzzle. His face still had the unhealthy gray pallor. He looked like he hadn't shaved in a while.

"How are you feeling, Mr. Smith?"

"I'm well, thank you, Detective Sloane. Hello, Detective Carr." He nodded at me. "Eleanor." He laid his paper aside. "The surgeons here are the best in the world. There's a reason. During the Civil War, when the practice of surgery was in its infancy, all the best doctors were drawn here to perform complicated procedures on uncomplaining subjects. To sharpen their scalpel techniques." He giggled at his own joke.

Walt sounded like his usual self, explaining how a watch works.

"Did you know that the first operation on the abdomen for a pistol shot wound was performed here in 1894? They've had plenty of practice since, so my case was quite simple for them.

They patched me right up. By the way, Eleanor, I harbor no ill feelings."

Sloane placed a recorder on the bedside table. "Glad to hear you're recovering. Can we ask you some questions?"

Walt gestured toward aluminum side chairs. "Ask away."

We pulled the chairs next to the bed, and Sloane pushed Start on the recorder. "This is an interview with Walter Smith. Present are Detectives Sloane and Carr and an observer, Eleanor Tracy." He checked his watch. "The time is oh-nine-eighteen. The date is January fifteenth. Mr. Smith, you have been read your rights. Do you understand you have a right to an attorney at this interview?"

"I do, and I decline."

"Ms. Tracy is here as an observer. Do you agree to that?"

"Of course my friend Eleanor is welcome. I expect she'll write the final installment to our saga."

Sloane checked the recorder. "Detectives from the Port Chester area will be visiting you later this week. Today, we'll be talking about three cases Detective Carr and I are investigating here in New York City. First, Judge John Hawthorne. Were you acquainted with Judge Hawthorne?"

Walt tapped his finger on his lips and scratched the stubble on his chin. "That is a difficult question, Detective. I suppose some would say we had the most intimate acquaintance two humans can have. But can you be more specific?"

This would take a while.

Sloane shifted in his chair. "When did you first meet Judge Hawthorne?"

"I was a reporter in his courtroom many years ago during the bribery trial of one James J. Coogan. But most recently, several months ago, I began observing the judge's court routinely. I introduced myself during a break in the proceedings after a few weeks. Aside from my taking a few photos of the judge, that was our last interaction, until that night, of course."

"Which night is that, Mr. Smith?"

"November fifteenth."

"Tell us about the night of November fifteenth.

"I waited across the street until the courthouse emptied around five thirty. The judge's clerk was one of the very last people to leave. I found my way to his chambers. The judge was quite a self-confident person. I suppose one has to be when it's your job to decide the fates of the people who appear before you. He thought he could talk me out of my plan to hang him."

Sloane and Carr exchanged glances.

"We had quite a long and interesting discussion about crime and punishment, and whether debts incurred in the past can be wiped clean by retribution in the present. He took the position that descendants are not responsible for the sins of their ancestors, which I found ironic since the evidence to the contrary is clearly there in the Bible. He talked the whole time, even as I tied his hands behind his back, made him climb on the chair, and put the noose over his head. He thought if he went along, he could convince me to relent. He didn't account for the knockout injection, of course. I pulled the rope tight, injected him, knocked the chair over, and tacked the note to his chest. You know the rest."

"You say you injected the judge."

"Yes, with propofol. I had no wish to watch him suffer." Walt held up a finger. "One moment, Detective." He rooted around under the sheet and found a button device attached by a long tube to an IV bag hanging at the head of his bed. "Have you seen these gadgets? They're experimental at the moment. I'm happy to be a guinea pig. They allow the patient, me in this case, to administer his own morphine without bothering the nurses. Quite ingenious." He closed his eyes and took several deep breaths. "Much better. Carry on."

"Where did you get the propofol?"

"Come now, Detective. You of all people must know with enough money one can buy almost anything in Times Square."

"Did you write a letter to Miss Tracy the next day after the judge's death?"

"Yes, after I read Harry Logan's story." Walt smiled my way. "I've had my eye on Eleanor since she joined our happy little band of reporters. She's a fine journalist, not willing to settle for expedient answers. She's the best one to tell our story."

I wanted to yell, "It's not our story," but I managed to hold my tongue.

Sloane turned over the tape and consulted his little spiral notebook. "Let's talk about November twentieth. Where were you around seven in the evening?"

"On the top floor of Six Sixty-six Fifth Avenue."

"Tell us about that night."

"Around six thirty, I entered the construction zone through a side gate someone had carelessly left unlocked and rode the elevator to the top floor. Quite rickety."

Amen to that.

"I knew it was Mr. Putnam's habit to inspect progress on the job every weeknight at about seven o'clock, almost always alone. True to form, he showed up. I heard the elevator rattle to a stop, and he stepped off in his construction worker costume: jeans, flannel shirt, and hard hat. I waited till he turned his back to consult some blueprints, then injected him."

"With the propofol."

"Yes."

Sloane pulled a folded paper from his pocket. "This is a copy of a letter addressed to Miss Tracy that describes the murder of Tommy Putnam. Did you write this letter, Mr. Smith?"

Walt took it, read it, and nodded.

"Please answer aloud for the tape."

"Yes, I wrote this letter and delivered it to Eleanor's apartment."

"Will you read it aloud, please."

Walt read the letter and waited for the next question.

"You crushed Tommy Putnam to death under a pile of cinder blocks?"

"Yes, just as Giles Corey, an innocent man, was crushed to death in Salem Village in 1692. He was wrongly accused by the Putnams of being a witch, and he refused to admit to the lie. The Putnam family has a long history of grasping for money and power on the backs of innocent people, even to the present. I heard His admonition to me very clearly. 'Prepare slaughter for his children for the iniquity of their fathers; that they do not rise, nor possess the land, nor fill the face of the world with cities.'"

Sloane squirmed in his chair and closed his book. "Let's take a break, Mr. Smith." He looked at his watch. "Interview paused at ten ten." He pushed Stop on the recorder and led Christine and me out of the room and down the hall to a small waiting area. "You heard him say some supernatural voice gave the murder order. He's trying to set up an insanity defense with the business about 'He told me to do it.' I need to ask him about the Bible quotes, but I'm afraid it will play right into his hands."

I spoke up. "What if he really is crazy?"

"I'll leave it to his defense lawyer to make that case. I don't want to make it for him."

We trouped back into Walt's room and sat down. Sloane started the recorder again. "Interview with Walter Smith resumed at ten fifteen. Let's move on to the night of January second. A fire destroyed the office of Dr. William Griggs and ultimately led to his demise. Did you start that fire, Mr. Smith?"

"I did."

"You described your actions that night on a phone call with Miss Tracy. You flooded the doctor's office with oxygen in the confined space of his records room and lit a spark that set off the fire. What was your connection with Dr. Griggs?"

"I met him for the first time on the night of January second. I had observed his movements for a few weeks, but I had never met him before that night." He tented his fingers. "In a funny way, I felt I knew his ancestor, Dr. William Griggs, who lived almost four hundred years ago, much more intimately than I did the present-day Dr. Griggs. Dr. Griggs of 1690 started the whole Salem witch hysteria. Present-day Dr. Griggs's death settled that evil debt."

"Let's move on. You've been arrested on charges of murder of John Hawthorne, Thomas Putnam, Jr., and William Griggs, Jr., plus kidnapping and false imprisonment of Christine Carr."

"Yes, and I apologize, Detective Carr for the, uh..." He gestured toward the back of his head. "Entirely inadvertent."

Christine fingered the bandage as though she had forgotten about it.

"Before Detective Carr appeared on the scene, I expected Dr. Griggs would be the end of my story of retribution. Imagine my surprise. Her distant relative, Ann Carr Putnam, played a primary role in accusations against Reverend George Burroughs that led to his trial and execution. Sadly, my mission will be incomplete. No offense, Detective Carr."

Sloane slammed his book shut. "Interview terminated at ten thirty."

He turned off the recorder and gathered it up. We left the room single file. Outside, Sloane rubbed the back of his neck. "I couldn't listen to it anymore. We've got enough, anyway. We've got means, motive, and opportunity for the three murders and your abduction. The rest of it is just his crazy ravings."

Christine seemed to wilt before our eyes. "I need to sit down for a minute."

We led her to a couch in the waiting area, and I got her a cup of water at the fountain.

"This is an order, Carr. Take a few days off. I'll get this tape back to the station and carry things for a while. My first call is going to be to the commissioner. He can climb down off my back now."

We shared a cab uptown and they dropped me at the paper. I sat at my desk to write the next installment of The Avenger case.

"Excuse me." A copyboy who was actually a girl was standing in front of my desk. I had seen her around. She always seemed to be working harder than anyone else, and she stood out because she was about six feet tall. She was wearing a blazer with sleeves too short that looked like she had borrowed it.

"Yeah. I'm working on it. Give me about half an hour."

She didn't leave. She stuck out her hand. "Ah, I'm Jamie Baker, Miss Tracy. I'm the new Dear Aunt Betty and society reporter. I'm going to be sitting behind you right there." She pointed to Walt's desk.

"Is that so?"

I glanced at Duke's office. He and Harry were watching the interaction and grinning. Duke motioned me inside. "Have a seat, Butch. Harry and I have been talking, and we agree. How would you like a full-time crime assignment?"

"You know it." My audition for crime reporter was over.

Chapter Twenty-Three

A CHILLY BREEZE FLUTTERED the sheer curtains that framed open windows. Gene and David generally keep their apartment too cold for my taste. I tease them they could hang meat in their living room if they ever took a notion. They keep an afghan David's grandma knitted draped across the back of the couch just for me. I love those boys.

Gene got up to stir his spaghetti sauce and refill our wineglasses.

David raised his glass in a toast. "Here's to the newest *Gazette* crime-beat reporter, Butch Tracy. And I have a surprise. Here's to New York City's finest brand-new CPA, Eugene Welsh."

Christine and I yelled in unison, "You passed!" We grabbed hands and danced around the coffee table, chanting, "No more studying."

Christine flopped down on the couch. "I have a surprise too. The police doc cleared me for active duty, and you're looking at the official no-longer-on-probation Detective Christine Carr. I've been assigned to street crimes in Chinatown, narcotics and prostitution. I'll be working out of the Fifth. I report there tomorrow."

David said, "Back to the Fifth? You'll be working with Rollins again. Maybe Butch's role in solving the Kapoor and Avenger cases will have opened up his mind about professional women."

"Maybe, but I won't count on it. Butch has solved half a dozen cases for us. Pretty soon we're going to have to put her on the payroll."

"No thanks. I prefer to write about human drama, not police it."

Gene served up our spaghetti, and we dug in.

Christine moaned. "How does someone named Eugene Welsh make such fabulous Italian spaghetti?"

"A secret ingredient. I'll share it with you if you bring us up to speed on what's happening with the Walter Smith case."

"Deal. You first."

"The secret is adding a dash of red wine to the sauce just as it starts bubbling. Now about The Avenger. Has the coroner determined Smith's cause of death?"

Christine shook her head. "It's tricky. He could have accidentally overdosed himself on morphine, or he could have done it on purpose. Then there's the advanced prostate cancer."

"They found the Peale miniatures in his apartment, right?"

"Yes, the forensics techs found them stashed under a loose floorboard in his bedroom."

"Was he planning to sell them?"

"We'll never know. I suspect he thought he was saving them from the fire for posterity."

I sipped my wine. "Another thing we'll never know. My gut tells me he was descended from Reverend George Burroughs. The cops couldn't match the prints they lifted at the Griggs fire with any Walter Smith records. I think at some point he changed his identity. It wouldn't surprise me if he was Reverend Burroughs's great-grandson times nine or ten."

David leaned back from the table and patted his stomach. "That spaghetti was great, hon."

Gene began gathering the plates, and I got up to help him clear the table. "Sit. Sit. I'm just going to take these plates away to make room for our coffee. And so we can play a game of Clue."

David, Christine, and I groaned. "Not again. It's boring. You win every time."

Gene held up his hands. "Fine. Let's play something else then. How about Monopoly?"

"You'll win Monopoly too. How about Scrabble? Give us a chance."

Gene won the Scrabble game.

After the game, David covered a big yawn. "Excuse me, ladies. Gene, we better get to these dishes. You two relax. Go out and sit on the stoop and see if you can find some stars."

I took Christine's hand and led her out the front door to sit on the stone front steps. Pear trees line our street. In the spring and summer, they bear white clusters of tiny fragrant blossoms that make the trees look like giant puff balls. In the winter, their spindly bare branches cast lacy shadows on the sidewalk.

Christine wrapped her arms around her knees. "I'm starting to feel New York City is home. It's time I start seriously looking for an apartment. The Barbizon has been fine for my purposes, but I'll have to admit, the incident with Walter Smith has freaked me out. I certainly don't enjoy the pool the way I did before. I guess I got too comfortable down there. Smith was able to sneak up from behind and inject me with propofol before I knew what was happening. I could kick myself for that."

"How did he get down in the basement, with the Barbizon's no-men policy?"

"I think because the front desk was so focused on keeping men from the upper floors. Heaven forbid any of the girls might be carrying on in their rooms with their boyfriends. He probably took the stairs down from the lobby unchallenged."

Etta James singing "At Last" drifted from Gene and David's window. Christine put her arm around my shoulders and pulled me close. "This street is so nice."

"Wait till spring and the trees start to bloom."

"When I came to New York, I didn't know there would be trees. It's funny how your imagination draws pictures."

"Does your comfort with New York mean you're beginning to leave Buffalo behind? And Bella?"

"I haven't told you—Bella called the station looking for me a few days ago. I suppose she tracked me down through personnel records at Buffalo PD."

"What did she want?" I waited for "Please forgive me," or "Take me back," or "Come back to Buffalo."

Christine glanced sideways at me. "I didn't return the call, and I don't intend to."

A rush of relief surged through me. "We agreed to slow down to avoid professional conflicts. I think we did a good job in the Kapoor and The Avenger cases."

"So far we have. We're smart to take things one step at a time."

"I know you're right, but sometimes I feel like I'm auditioning for a relationship with you. I suppose I can live with that if the next step is you staying with me tonight."

She kissed me. "I can live with that."

David and Gene joined us on the stoop with more wine. David jumped up. "Hold on. We have to memorialize this moment." He ran into the apartment and came back with his camera and tripod. He set up the camera on the sidewalk, adjusted the timer, and scrambled into place. "Say cheese." The flashbulb popped.

In the weeks after the night of celebration with spaghetti, Christine combed the papers for apartment rentals, but she never seemed to find time to actually look at any places. Instead, she began staying more often with me, and she finally moved in for good in April when the pear trees were starting to bud.

Here we are nine and a half years later. The aroma of baking turkey and pecan pie is wafting up the stairway from David and Gene's apartment. That photo of the four of us on spaghetti night, young and smiling, sits on the table in our apartment, next to my police band radio.

THE END

About Jane Alden

Jane Alden was born and raised in a small Mississippi River Delta community in Arkansas. Everyone in town knew everyone else—their parents, and their grandparents before them. Though her father was a life-long cotton farmer, the family lived in town rather than on the farm, the only class difference in the all-white, all-protestant hamlet.

After graduating from the University of Arkansas, she moved to California and taught seventh grade English in a small central valley citrus-farming community. When she was recruited on the phone at U of A, she looked up Porterville, California, on the map, and it was only about an inch and a half north of Los Angeles, but it turned out the culture was closer to Arkansas or Oklahoma than to the bright lights and big city she craved. After two years teaching, she moved to Los Angeles and began a career in health care management. After many lucky circumstances and thanks to wonderful mentors, she ultimately became Chief Executive Officer at Los Angeles Children's Hospital, a mountain-top experience. After running a big organization for eight years, she became an executive coach, working with successful executives who want to be better leaders.

Jane and her partner of thirty years live in a small town thirty miles east of metropolitan Los Angeles. Claremont is rare for a Southern California town, having a distinct downtown village area and discernable city limits. Their chocolate lab, Delilah, is the captain of the domestic ship.

Visit Jane's website at janealden.com to chat about lesbian stories, our experiences, and other interesting things. 'Like" her on Facebook at Jane Alden, email Janealdenauthor@gmail.com.

Connect with Jane:
Email: janealdenauthor@gmail.com
Twitter: @janealden5
Facebook: JaneAldenBooks

Note to Readers:

Thank you for reading a book from Desert Palm Press. We appreciate you as a reader and want to ensure you enjoy the reading process. We would like you to consider posting a review on your preferred media sites and/or your blog or website.

For more information on upcoming releases, author interviews, contest, giveaways and more, please sign up for our newsletter and visit us as at Desert Palm Press: www.desertpalmpress.com and "Like" us on Facebook: Desert Palm Press.

Bright Blessings